Accidental Dad

Lois Richer

D0189914

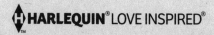

Recycling programs for this product may not exist in your area.

LOVE INSPIRED BOOKS

ISBN-13: 978-0-373-71942-6

Accidental Dad

Copyright © 2016 by Lois M. Richer

www.Harlequin.com

Printed in U.S.A.

Now glory be to God, who by His mighty power
at work within us is able to do far more than
we would ever dare to ask or even dream of—
infinitely beyond our highest prayers,
desires, thoughts, or hopes.
—*Ephesians* 3:20–21

"I can see you'll be an amazing father," Kelly said to Sam.

"It's obvious you love the kids, so I know your concern will be for them first, last and always."

"How do you know that?" Sam asked curiously, though pleased by her flattering assessment.

"It's there for anyone to see in everything you do with them," Kelly said. "You've sensed that Emma isn't herself so you're trying to figure out what's troubling her. I've watched you give Jacob Samuel extra attention when he's fussing, seen you rein in headstrong Sadie in a gentle but firm way." She leaned forward, utterly serious. "You are their father now, Sam, in every way that counts."

"Thank you." Sam's throat jammed at her generous words.

"This is where you belong, caring for them," Kelly said. "But I don't. I'll stay for six months. Then I have to go."

"Have to?" he asked softly.

"Yes." She sounded sad. "You have the ranch, your parents, the kids. They're an integral part of your world. They define you."

Sam's heart ached for her as she walked toward the door, a solitary figure.

Lois Richer loves traveling, swimming and quilting, but mostly she loves writing stories that show God's boundless love for His precious children. As she says, "His love never changes or gives up. It's always waiting for me. My stories feature imperfect characters learning that love doesn't mean attaining perfection. Love is about keeping on keeping on." You can contact Lois via email, loisricher@yahoo.com, or on Facebook (LoisRicherAuthor).

Books by Lois Richer

Love Inspired

Family Ties

A Dad for Her Twins
Rancher Daddy
Gift-Wrapped Family
Accidental Dad

Northern Lights

North Country Hero
North Country Family
North Country Mom
North Country Dad

Healing Hearts

A Doctor's Vow
Yuletide Proposal
Perfectly Matched

Love for All Seasons

The Holiday Nanny
A Baby by Easter
A Family for Summer

Visit the Author Profile page at Harlequin.com for more titles.

Chapter One

Sam Denver's mind wasn't on Valentine's Day or Canada's frosty winterscape outside the airport in Calgary, Alberta.

Thanks to a huge poster advertising tropical vacations, he was mentally immersed in the azure waters of the Mediterranean as it lapped against warm sandy beaches. Ocean breezes caressed his face, carrying the pungent whiff of salty brine and the cheerful whistle of nearby fishermen in small bobbing boats with white billowing sails as they hauled aboard their catches. He'd be thirty this year, and he couldn't remember a time when he hadn't dreamed of seeing the world.

"Flight 455 from Toronto has now arrived. Passengers will emerge at gate…"

The announcement ended Sam's reverie and drew him back to the cold, hard sting of reality.

Traveling the world now was as likely as sharing this romantic day with a sweetheart. But it was nowhere near as hard to let go of his travel dream as it was to let go of Jake, his twin, the best friend Sam had never been without. That aching void was compounded because Jake's beloved wife, Marina, had died in the car accident with him. Now Sam was alone to care for their infant son and almost-adopted twin girls.

The kids needed him. Marina's parents needed him. His own parents needed him. The ranch wouldn't survive without him. If Sam thought about it for very long, the weight of his responsibilities brought waves of trepidation. How could he possibly be what they all needed and still keep the Triple D running?

With help. From one passenger on flight 455.

Sam tilted back on his boots and studied the emerging travelers. Eager yet anxious about the upcoming meeting, he tossed out his half-full coffee cup and scanned features of each traveler as they passed by. None matched the face of the woman he remembered from almost ten years ago.

Nervousness built inside. Where was she? She would have cleared customs in Toronto. There should be no holdup here. He pulled out his phone and rechecked her email. Yes, this was the right flight, and there was no new message saying she'd been delayed. Maybe she wasn't coming?

Then a tall, slim woman appeared, and a rush of relief surged through Sam. Kelly Krause. He'd have known that tipped-up nose anywhere. Her glossy dark brown hair fell straight and thick to her shoulders, cupping her cheeks in a caress that emphasized high cheekbones and big dark eyes. For some reason his heart did a little giddyup.

A lot of time had passed since Sam had stood beside Kelly at the front of a church while his twin married hers, but she looked as beautiful now as she had then, except that her tanned olive skin bore signs of recent weeping, as did her red-rimmed eyes. She paused to scan the area before striding toward him.

Sam couldn't help noticing how well Kelly's jeans fit or that her peacock-blue shirt and matching sweater did great things for her figure. He tamped down his reaction. This was his sister-in-law. Yes, she was gorgeous, but anything beyond that was out of bounds for him. Sam didn't do relationships, not since Naomi. Still, as she moved toward him, he thought Kelly still looked young and vulnerable with her lime-green backpack swinging from one hand.

The answer to his dilemma had arrived. If Sam was a praying man he'd be asking for help to convince Kelly to stay. But he'd given up everything to do with God the day Naomi died, unable to reconcile the loving God he'd always believed in with the One who let his beloved fiancée suffer so terribly before dying of cancer at twenty-five. If God so loved, why hadn't He prevented— No!

He stepped forward as Kelly halted in front of him. Her gaze meshed with his.

"Hi, Sam." Her soft voice barely penetrated the happy din of reunited families around them.

"Hi, Kelly." He hugged her quickly then stepped back.

She tried to smile, her perfect, even teeth blazing white against the tan of her face. But then tears filled her eyes. "Oh, Sam."

"I know." He gulped, swallowing his own emotions to deal with the next step. That was the only way he could handle things right now. "Where's the rest of your luggage?"

"It will come later. The cruise line's sending it. I didn't want to wait. I just wanted to get here." She stopped suddenly, as if realizing that there was no point in rushing. Not now.

"I'm glad you did." Kelly's weary demeanor told Sam she was worn out by her long flight from Europe. "Would you like to stop for a coffee or something to eat before we head to the ranch?"

"How far is it?" she asked. "Marina never—" She gulped as tears returned to roll down her smoothly sculpted cheeks. "I'm sorry," she whispered helplessly.

Sam knew exactly how she felt. He wanted to bawl himself, but he kept rigid control of his emotions because the kids needed him to make everything okay in their world.

"Come on," he said gently. He slid an arm around her

shoulders, ignoring the flutter in his stomach when his hand brushed her warm skin. "Let's get a coffee. There's no hurry." He thought of the almost ten years of Jake and Marina's marriage when Kelly could have visited and didn't. But what did the past matter now? They had the future to deal with. "Was the trip okay?"

She shook her head. "Bumpy from Toronto. I didn't feel well."

"But you're okay now?" Relieved when she nodded, Sam said, "So maybe you need breakfast. You sit here and I'll get it."

Sam waited until she was seated then strode to the counter. He ordered two breakfast sandwiches, hash browns and two cups of coffee, even though he didn't want anything to eat or more caffeine. He wanted to get back to the ranch, to get busy with something, anything that would dull the pain and take his mind off his loss. But sharing a meal might help Kelly relax, so he'd go through the motions. He carried the loaded tray back to her and pretended to relish unwrapping his food.

Kelly ate daintily, carefully, but she finished only half her sandwich and just a bite of the hash brown before pushing away her tray and leaning back in her chair, her coffee cup pressed against her cheek as if she craved the warmth it offered.

"Sam Denver the Fixerator," she murmured with a tiny smile that didn't quite make it to her sad eyes. "How are you, Sam?"

"I'm okay." He shrugged and would have let it go, but Kelly raised an eyebrow and tilted her head forward, obviously unsatisfied with his brief answer. "Dad hasn't been that well, and since Jake's death—" He swallowed, struggling to get past that awful word.

"You've taken over, huh?" Kelly nodded as if she understood the pressure he was under. "Well, if anyone can manage it, I'm sure you can." She frowned at the table-top then lifted her gaze to meet his. "Sam, I phoned home several times but nobody answered. Do you know where my parents—"

"They're at the ranch." He chided himself for not inform-ing her earlier. "I should have told you in my email, but I figured you had enough on your plate just getting here, and I didn't want to add to your worries."

"Something's wrong, isn't it?" she asked in a tight voice.

"Yes." Sam hated watching her lose the calm that had barely begun to ease her weary posture. "Kelly, your dad was recently diagnosed with Alzheimer's."

Her back went rigid. "But—" She stopped, unable to voice her thoughts, her face appalled.

"I was in Victoria on business and I stopped by to see them," he continued. "I could see something was off with him and that your mom was struggling, but she wouldn't admit to me that anything was wrong."

Kelly's nod told him she understood what he wasn't say-ing, that Arabella Krause was not a woman to be easily persuaded of anything.

"Go on," she whispered, her expression showing stark fear.

"With Marina's help, I convinced her to take your dad to the doctor. I went to my conference then stopped by to see them again. The tests had worn out both of them so I invited them to come to the ranch and stay with Marina while they waited for results. Vancouver Island was too far away for her to help them. We only heard the diagno-sis shortly before…"

"No one told me." Her lips tightened. Her dark eyes flashed at him angrily. "Why?"

"You haven't exactly kept in touch, Kelly." Sam veered away from that, refusing to issue blame. She had enough to deal with. "Marina was going to email you about it but then the twins' adoptions—you know about the twin girls they fostered and were trying to adopt after the mother died?"

"Yes. Marina seemed ecstatic about it." Kelly's forehead pleated. "But I thought the adoption would have been completed by now. They had the twins for what—a year?"

"Almost." Sam shrugged. "They had to allow time to search for family. Only after that was complete could the adoption process proceed. Marina and Jake were coming to Calgary to make their final case before the judge." This part was so hard to say, so hard to accept. He'd given Kelly the bare facts about their deaths in his email, but it was time she knew the details. He cleared his throat, but that didn't erase the wobble in his voice. "A semi-truck lost control on black ice and hit them head-on. They died instantly."

When Sam finally looked up, his breath caught in his throat. Kelly's face had paled to ashen white. Her tear-filled gaze darted around as if she was searching for something, anything, to make the horror of their deaths understandable. He knew a thousand questions were tumbling through her mind, most of all, *Why?* He knew that because he'd asked himself the same thing over and over. And never found an answer that satisfied.

"Where were the kids?" she choked when she was finally able to squeeze out the words.

"At home with my parents." He smiled, hoping to ease her anxiety. "They're fine."

No, they weren't. Five-year-old twins Emma and Sadie were lost and confused. They couldn't understand why their Mommy and Daddy didn't come kiss them good-night. And six-month-old Jacob Samuel, upset by everyone else's turmoil, cried for familiar arms to rock him to sleep.

"Thank God they're okay," Kelly managed to say on a broken sniffle. She dislodged her tears with her fingertips, though more quickly followed. "I keep asking God why He allowed this. They were so happy. Marina seemed to adore the twins, and then she finally had the baby she'd longed for since they were married. Her emails made it sound like everything was perfect. So why?"

Since Sam didn't have an answer, he remained silent.

"So you're saying the girls aren't Denvers. Is that right?" Kelly stared at him as she waited for a response.

"No." Sam hated that admission. The twins were Denvers in every way that mattered.

"Marina never gave me the details about how they came to be at the ranch," Kelly said softly. "Would you mind explaining?"

"Sure." Sam couldn't deny her the information, but man, it hurt to go back to those halcyon days. He steeled himself against emotion and laid out the facts. "Abby Lebret owns Family Ties, an adoption agency in Buffalo Gap. Calgary Children's Services contacted her to see if she could find the twins a home where they could live while their mother underwent chemotherapy. She asked Jake and Marina. Sadly, the mother died. Since the twins' father was married with a family and had disowned them and the girls were by then very much at home on the Triple D, not to mention that our siblings had come to adore the twins, Abby helped Marina and Jake petition the court for adoption."

"Poor kids but fortunate to have Jake and Marina," Kelly mused, her gaze far away.

"Yes. They went all out to make a home for them." Sam fought for composure. Even though he'd had five days to adjust, the loss of the lively couple still seemed so surreal. "That day the twins were sick. Marina didn't want to leave them, and Abby couldn't persuade the judge to come to Buffalo Gap, so—"

"Jake and Marina went to Calgary to see the judge," she finished. "I'm guessing my sister couldn't wait to officially become their mother." Kelly managed a small smile when Sam nodded.

"They wanted things finalized." Would he ever forget that horrific phone call?

"I see." Kelly paused, blinked away the moisture in her eyes then asked, "But there's no issue with you adopting the twins, right?" She frowned when he didn't answer and touched his sleeve. "Sam?"

"Since the adoption decree wasn't registered before Jake's and Marina's deaths, Children's Services has applied to the court to regain custody citing concerns that Sadie and Emma no longer have parents or a proper home." He cleared his throat. "Since I went through the foster parent training classes with Jake and Marina, Abby begged the judge to let the girls stay with me at the ranch while I apply to adopt them. Abby thought you and I being named as guardians of the three children might influence his decision."

"I understand them naming you." Kelly's dismay was the last thing Sam wanted to hear. "But why me?"

"Because you're Marina's sister, and because they knew neither of our parents are well enough to care for three active kids." Sam inhaled, hoping she'd understand. "It's up to you and me to keep this family together, Kelly."

"But I know nothing about kids," she protested, obviously taken aback. "And I can't be their guardian for long. I have a job I have to return to."

"When I was trying to locate you, the cruise line told me you're going on leave for six months." Irritated that she considered her job as a port consultant more important than her family, Sam blurted, "Are you willing to see your sister's children raised by someone else?"

"No, but you don't understand." Poor Kelly looked confused and lost.

Sam's heart ached for her. Part of him wanted to gather her in his arms and comfort her. He knew the loss of Jake and Marina had hit Kelly as hard as it had him, maybe harder, because she hadn't seen her twin in so long. But the other part of Sam wanted to demand Kelly stop holding her grudge or whatever it was that had kept her away all these years and act like part of the family. Because she was.

He hadn't expected Kelly's refusal but perhaps he should have. Marina had told him how hard Kelly had worked to move up in the industry. He'd known Marina occasionally sent Kelly newsy emails about her life, their parents and her growing family. He'd admired his sister-in-law for trying to include Kelly as part of the family, for trying to build a bridge. But other than sending a Christmas package every year, Kelly had stayed away and maintained only sporadic contact.

At this moment, though, Sam didn't care that Kelly had left home the night of Jake and Marina's wedding, nor did it matter to him what had kept her away all this time. All he knew was that he desperately needed her help to keep his family together.

"Don't you see?" Sam asked. "Both our parents are living at the ranch because they can't manage on their own. My dad had another heart attack, your dad has Alzheimer's, the kids need stability and someone has to run the ranch to support everyone. I daren't let any one of those balls drop, or we'll be in trouble."

"I know it hasn't been easy, Sam. You've done a great job." Kelly smiled sadly. "Thank you for caring for my parents and the kids."

"I managed," he said, irritated that she didn't yet seem to get it. "But we have to do more than that if the twins are to stay. The ranch is the kids' future, the legacy Jake wanted to leave them. I can't let my brother down. I won't let the ranch or the twins go without a fight." He stared into her eyes and laid out his case. "It's up to you and me to keep the family together, Kelly. That's what Jake and Marina wanted. That's why they named us guardians."

Kelly remained silent for a long time, studying him with

her teary brown eyes, confused and heartrendingly sad. Finally, she murmured, "Sam?"

"Yes?" He knew she was going to ask something important because of the way she stared at him, ready to assess his response. He knew this answer mattered a lot to her from the way she bit her bottom lip and how her hands fiddled with her cup. "What is it, Kelly?"

"Was Marina happy?" Her voice cracked, a world of sorrow, guilt and heartache underneath the words.

At least that question was easily answered. He nodded. "Marina and Jake were very happy," he assured her.

"I'm glad," she whispered. Then her control shattered, and she wept her heart out.

And that was when Sam did what his head told him not to. He got up from his chair, walked to hers and gently eased Kelly into his arms. Ignoring the sudden rush of his heartbeat, he drew her close and brushed a hand against her hair, offering the only thing he had to give—comfort. He couldn't pray, couldn't ask God to make it better. God had let his brother die, just like Naomi.

All Jake could do was hope his support would help lovely Kelly Krause surmount her grief enough to help him rebuild their family.

For the first time in years Kelly relaxed her rigid control on her life and let Sam support her as she cried for the sister she hadn't seen in years. Why had she let her mother keep her away so long? Why had she let her embarrassment over a crush on Jake that was almost ten years old and her mother's cruel words and harsh judgments drive a wedge between her and her twin?

As Sam held her, Kelly felt an old stirring rise inside. The strength in his embrace comforted her. His compassion as he led her away from the eatery and to an upholstered bench also rekindled a long-suppressed yearning inside to belong to someone, to be cherished. But that was silly. Sam was just a friend, a brother-in-law who was trying to help her cope. She couldn't let herself imagine there was more than kindness in his actions.

He eased her onto the bench and sat down beside her. His arm across her shoulders felt right, like a kind of bond that drew them together. Finally, she managed to smile at him.

"Sorry," Kelly apologized. "It hits me that she's gone and I won't ever see her again, and that's when the tears start."

"I know." He handed her a fresh tissue and waited while she dried her eyes.

"How do you handle it?" she asked, curious about his steely strength. Like her, he had lost a twin, a brother whom she knew he loved.

"There's so much to do. I focus on juggling things to keep everyone else going," Sam told her, his voice bald with pain.

"Sam the Fixerator." Kelly smiled at the moniker, remembering the fondness in Marina's voice when she'd first introduced him with that title. "Still trying to fix things, Sam?" A second later she wished she could retract the words. He couldn't fix this. No one could.

"It's all I know to do." Sam shrugged then checked his watch. "If you're ready, we should get on the road."

When Kelly didn't immediately respond, he touched her hand. A zap of awareness tingled up her arm at the contact. Why was it that Sam had this strange effect on her? She drew away then slowly rose and took her backpack from him.

"I'm sure there are many things to do." Her breath caught, but she pushed through the pain. "When are the funerals?"

"We were waiting for you," he said quietly. "We can start planning now that you're home."

Home? Kelly had never been to Triple D Ranch, and

yet she found the thought of staying where Marina had found such joy oddly attractive. She hadn't had her own place in so long. Her parents were staying on the Triple D, too. Would Marina's ranch house be the place where she and her mom could finally move beyond their bitter past? Could she really come home?

Only, Kelly knew, if she could get rid of the guilt, guilt that, if her mother knew she felt, would use to condemn her, as she'd so often done in the past. Not that her mother would have to say a word. Inside Kelly's head, a voice reminded, *Your sister, your twin, is dead, and you never told her you loved her. You never said goodbye.*

"Time to leave, Kelly." Sam's quiet voice stirred her from her misery. His gaze scanned her from head to foot. "You need a warmer jacket. I'll buy one from that store over there."

"I already have one." Kelly unzipped her backpack and pulled out the quilted coat she'd often worn to ski in the Alps. He held it so she could slide her arms into it, and again feelings of being cared for, cherished, welled up. "I'll be fine. Let's go," she said, anxious to escape his touch and her strange reactions to it.

Sam studied her coat with a dubious glance but nodded, and they left the airport.

They fought their way through the icy wind racing across the parkade to his truck.

"I should have said it before. I'm so sorry about Jake."

"I know." For a moment, steady, organized Sam looked utterly bereft.

In that instant Kelly noticed the few silver hairs in his sideburns and the tiny fan of lines around his green eyes that hadn't been there when she'd last seen him. Ten years ago Sam had been a very handsome man, and time hadn't changed that. But grief had stolen what she'd privately labeled his "cowboy" smile, a lopsided twist of his lips she'd never seen copied. Still, Kelly thought she saw a hint of it now in his soft smile.

"Inside the truck, Kelly," he insisted. "Don't think I can't see that you're freezing in that coat."

She climbed inside gratefully, huddling in her jacket while trying to hide just how chilled she felt. Sam slammed her door shut, hurried around to the other side and got in the driver's seat. Though he'd started the truck remotely, it hadn't yet warmed. The chill, combined with her apprehension at the upcoming meeting with her mother, made Kelly frown.

Sam studied her as if trying to read her mind. "Is something wrong?"

"No." She forced a smile. "I was wondering how long the ride will take."

"I forgot you've never been to the Triple D. Forty-five minutes or so. Mom will be feeding the kids lunch soon, and then Jacob Samuel will go down for his nap." His voice dropped as he drove out of the city. "I hope she gets a chance to relax and enjoy a cup of coffee."

"She's not well?" Kelly asked, barely remembering Jake's parents as a cheerful couple at Marina's wedding.

"She's worn out from caring for Dad and the twins and Jacob Samuel," he said, a deep fondness lacing his words. "Mom tries to do everything."

"I guess that's who you take after." Kelly grinned at his dour look then frowned. "Surely my mom's helping her?" She realized how silly that was the moment she said it. Her mother had never been particularly fond of children. "You said she and my dad are living at the ranch?"

"My parents are at my place. Yours are at Marina and Jake's. They were visiting when—" He didn't finish that. "Your mother is pretty much tied down with your dad. With his memory failing more frequently, he needs someone around all the time." Sam paused and glanced at her then said in a quiet voice, "I should warn you—he may not recognize you."

"The disease has progressed that far?" Sam's solemn nod made her catch her breath.

"Thank you for coming to get me," she said, finally grasping the extent of his responsibilities. "I'm sure it was a nuisance for you to drive all the way in to Calgary then back."

"I had to," Sam said with a smile, and when Kelly arched a questioning eyebrow, he replied, "You're part of the family. We need you with us."

So few words and yet they meant so much to her. *Part of the family.* Somewhere inside her, the words fanned long-buried embers of wanting to belong into a tiny flame. Could she finally belong?

Until she had to leave.

When Sam said, "Tell me what you were doing in Rome, Kelly," she suddenly remembered his solemn words to her on the patio the night of the wedding.

Someday, Kelly, I am going to see the birthplace of the Olympic Games. I will go to England and walk around Stonehenge. I'll stand and gaze at the fjords of Norway. I'll visit the hill in Turkey where the Apostle John is said to have taken Mary to live out her last days. I am going. It's just a matter of when.

She wondered if he'd ever managed to see any of them.

"Were you scouting out new places for tours?" he asked.

"Sort of. When I return from this leave, I'm to be transferred. I hope to Indonesia. I was going to go there next week…" She let the words die away when a grimness flickered across his face at her mention of the future.

"What exactly does a port consultant do?" he asked.

"What *I* do is become so familiar with our ship's ports of call that when a guest asks me about one of them, I'm able to recommend ways for them to see as much of the place as possible in their limited time. Or I suggest places that are a bit off the beaten track or that feature a particular interest of theirs. Whatever I can do to make their trip more memorable, that's what I am there for."

"Sounds like a calling," he said, tossing her a smile.

"That's how I feel about it." She shrugged. "Always have. When I started, I made it a point to intimately know each port where the ship docked, even though my first tour was to Alaska, and lots of the guests had been there before. I wanted to be able to direct any passenger who asked me for help. Mostly, they came back raving about the places I'd suggested they see. That got back to my superiors, and I received promotions. So I kept doing it."

"The night of the wedding—you talked a lot about traveling then," he said.

"I remember you did, too." She'd often replayed their conversation from the summer night they'd sat under the stars while everyone else danced at Jake and Marina's wedding. The strength of Sam's long-cherished dream to see the world, his clear, focused determination, still stuck in her mind.

As they rolled down the highway, Kelly blushed, remembering how natural it had seemed to share confidences on that perfect night. After Sam had revealed his soul-deep longing to travel, she'd blurted out her own painful story of meeting the man she was certain God meant for her, only to have him fall for someone else. Sam, being Sam, had comforted her, assuring her that God had someone special in mind for her. She'd felt so privileged to be in his confidence that night. Now she wondered if Sam had ever confided the depth of his desire to travel to anyone else.

She'd garnered from Marina's emails that Sam had postponed his plans to travel on at least four occasions "for the good of the family." As far as Kelly knew, he'd never left the ranch. Probably never would, now that he was responsible for it. Her heart bumped with affection. Dependable, loyal Sam, who willingly gave up his dreams for the ones he loved.

They drove in silence for a while. Kelly absorbed the beauty of the area where her sister had lived, immediately attracted to the gently sloping hills that grew to snow-capped mountains in the distance. Thick stands of ever-greens dotted the snowy landscape. Here and there cattle stood in pastures near massive bales of hay. Then the truck crested a hill, and a quaint little town spread before them.

"This is Buffalo Gap," Sam told her as they drove through the community. "That's the church where—" He paused, gulped. "Where Marina and Jake attended," he finally managed.

Kelly wondered at his angry look.

"About five thousand people live here. Not a big place, but it has most everything we need," he continued after a moment's pause. "Not far now to the Triple D."

They passed through Buffalo Gap, then at the top of another hill Sam turned left onto a gravel road and drove past several homes on either side. Then he turned right.

"Here we are." Sam drove under a big black metal arch with *Triple D* scripted above it. He grinned at her, obviously happy to be home, as a dimple appeared in one cheek. "We made good time."

Kelly checked her watch. The watch Marina had given her as a bridesmaid's gift.

Tears welled, and of course Sam wanted to know why. When she told him, he held out his own wrist and told her the watch he wore had been Jake's gift to him.

"They were quite a pair, our twins," he mused quietly.

"They were." Kelly blinked hard, forcing away her tears to concentrate on the upcoming meeting with her parents and Marina's kids.

Sam pulled up in front of a big white house with lattice

work around the eaves. Two lopsided snowmen dotted the front yard. Kelly knew this had been Marina's home. There was a wide front porch that would be perfect for sitting on long summer evenings and bright green flower boxes hanging from the railings—empty now, but Kelly could visualize brilliant blooms tumbling from them. Memories of a young Marina tending her flower garden played through her mind like an old movie. Her throat clogged as she fought back emotion.

"Relax, Kelly. No one's going to yell at you," Sam teased.

"How well do you know my mother, Sam?" Kelly managed to toss him a wry smile before she slid out of the truck. Inside, her stomach danced with nervousness. Would her dad know her? Would her mother launch one of her verbal attacks in front of Sam's parents—if they were there? Would the kids like her?

Sam slid his hand into hers and murmured, "We'll do this together."

Grateful for his support, Kelly clung to his hand as they walked the snowy path to the door and prayed for wisdom to get through the meeting with her mother.

Despite Sam's earlier welcome, Kelly doubted this could ever be her home. This was where Marina had belonged. Kelly was just a stand-in, the person her sister and Jake had chosen to help Sam keep the family dream alive. Could she do that?

Sam turned the knob, pushed open the door then stepped back, his green gaze holding hers with a tenderness that said he understood. Perhaps his "Welcome home, Kelly," was what gave her the strength to let go of his hand and step inside.

Chapter Two

"Hi, Mom. Dad." After hugging her parents, Kelly stood back, a tentative smile curving her full lips.

Sam figured he was probably the only one who saw a question lingering in the depths of her brown gaze and knew she wondered if her father's disease meant he wouldn't recognize her.

"Hey, Kelly." Neil Krause grinned at his daughter then hugged her again. "Boy, I'm glad to see you, honey. We've missed you so much."

"It took this to bring you home?" Arabella Krause wasn't as forgiving of her daughter's long absence. Sam winced at the anger underlying her snippy words.

"I'm sorry I didn't get back earlier, Mom." Kelly touched Arabella's cheek in the merest graze of her fingertips. She leaned forward and pressed a kiss there then pulled back to glance at the child wiggling in her mother's arms. "Who's this fellow?"

"That's Jacob Samuel Denver. He doesn't talk yet." A little girl with bright blond pigtails and cornflower blue eyes stood in front of Kelly. "I'm Sadie and this is my sister, Emma," she said, indicating her twin. "You're our mommy's sister, aren't you? But our mommy's not here anymore. She's gone." Big fat tears trickled down her cheeks.

"She's with God," Emma said in the whisper-soft voice she'd used ever since Sam had told the twins of their parents' deaths. She slipped her hand into Sadie's. "You're s'posed to be happy, Sadie. Mommy tol' us that's a happy place, 'member?"

"I don't want Mommy and Daddy to be gone," Sadie snapped. "I want them here."

Sam stepped forward to console her, but Kelly beat him to it.

"They are here, darling." Sam's heart blocked his throat as Kelly crouched down to the twins' level. "Your mom and dad are right here in your heart." She tapped Sadie's little chest. "They'll always be there because they loved you so much and because you loved them."

Sadie frowned. "Are you sure?"

"Yep. Positive," Kelly said with no hesitation. Sam could have hugged her for that when Sadie's sad tears immediately stopped.

"Oh." Sadie leaned forward until her lips were next to Kelly's ear. "I like talkin' 'bout my Mommy an' Daddy but it makes Grannybell cry." The not-quite-whispered words pierced the room's sudden silence.

Sam winced at Arabella's indrawn breath and tensed. Now Kelly's mother would take offense. She'd done a lot of that lately. To save everyone's nerves he prepared to intervene, but once again Kelly spoke first.

"Your mommy was Grannybell's daughter, Sadie. That means she was Grannybell's little girl, just like you and Emma are Mommy's very special little girls." Kelly's voice lost its composure for an instant, but she swallowed and quickly regained her poise. "You loved your mommy very much, right?" Two blond heads nodded. "Well, so did Grannybell."

"She doesn't like it that our mommy's with God?" Emma asked in the soft, hesitant voice Sam had begun to hate, because he hadn't been able to figure out how to cure it. Eyes wide, Emma risked a sideways glance at Arabella. "Why?"

"She likes Mommy to be with God," Kelly assured her. "But she misses Mommy very much, and sometimes that makes her cry. But it's okay for Grannybell to cry, and it's okay for you guys to talk about your mom and dad." Kelly nodded at their wide-eyed stares. "Talking about Mommy is how we remember her."

"Are you gonna talk 'bout her?" Sadie, the chatterbox, asked. "Uncle Sam tol' us you and Mommy were twins like me an' Emma."

"We were, only we didn't look like each other, like you two do." Kelly's voice wobbled. She cleared her throat then held out one hand. "I'm Auntie Kelly. Pleased to meet you, Miss Sadie. And you, Miss Emma."

Sam's lips twitched as the girls, bemused at being called *Miss*, each shook hands with their aunt.

"What about Jacob Samuel?" Emma asked, her voice barely above a whisper. "Don't you gotta shake hands with him, too?"

"He's just a baby. He doesn't shake hands," Sadie scolded.

"How do you do, Master Jacob Samuel Denver?" Kelly performed a bow in front of the little boy then took his tiny hand and shook it. "I'm very pleased to make your—ooh." She glanced at her hand, made a face then wiped her fingers on her pant leg amid the twins' giggles.

"Jacob Samuel drools," Sadie informed her.

"A lot," Emma added.

"Thank you. I'll remember that." Kelly looked around, taking in Marina's kitchen, her home. She suddenly looked so lost, Sam felt a rush of pity.

"Do you two want to see what I brought for you?" he asked the twins.

Sadie yelled "yes" and both girls jumped up and down

with excitement. No doubt he'd hear about their unseemly behavior from Arabella later, but for now their happy excitement sounded like music to Sam's ears. He handed them each a box, received a hug and then watched as the girls opened their gifts, dolls he'd bought in the airport store, oohing and ahhing over them as they lifted them free of the tissue paper while Kelly stood watching with a smile on her face.

"Arabella, this is for you and Neil. A small token to say thanks for helping my parents with the kids." He took the baby from her in trade for a huge box of the brand of candy he knew she favored. "Where are my parents, by the way?"

"At your father's medical appointment. Your mother thought it best to keep to his schedule," Arabella said in quiet tones, her gaze on Kelly.

"I think so, too," Sam agreed, relieved to see that nothing had happened while he was away. "So what's been happening?"

"Oscar said we got two new babies in the barn, Uncle Sam." Emma was entranced by the ranch animals.

"Where did you see Oscar?" he asked sharply. Hadn't Arabella been watching? Surely the twins hadn't gone out to the barn—fear crept up his spine.

"I seed him when me an' Sadie builded our snowmen," Emma murmured. "We got carrots for the noses an' I used one of your hats. Grannybell said it was 'propri—'" She frowned and turned to her twin. "What was that word?"

"I dunno." Sadie was too busy removing the clothes from her doll to even look up.

"Appropriate?" Kelly asked with an amused wink at Sam.

"Yeah." After Sam told her he had indeed noticed their snowman's hat, Emma crouched down beside her sister, and the two immediately launched into playtime.

"What do they call your mother?" Kelly asked curiously.

"Gran," he said and winked. "As opposed to Granny-bell for your mom."

"Cute." As Kelly glanced around, he noticed her back-pack still lay at her feet.

"Come on. I'll show you where you can stow your stuff." He picked up the pack and led the way to the back bed-room, next to the twins'. "Is this okay?" he asked, wishing he'd thought of dusting the spare room. "Your parents have the master bedroom. Marina thought it was easier for them with the attached bath."

"This is fine." She glanced around once, then her gaze returned to him. "You said your parents are staying here, too?"

"No, they're at my place." He walked to the window, drew back the curtain and pointed. "Over there. See?" he said with a burst of pride swelling inside at the log struc-ture he'd built mostly by himself from felling the trees to choosing the admittedly masculine decor. "They were in a place in town, sort of a practice run before buying a condo in the city, but it was too far away. This is better. I can check on them anytime."

"Good idea." Kelly's focus seemed to be on the empty walls.

"Something wrong?" he asked.

"Just wondering why Marina never hung anything in here." She shrugged. "The walls are all blank. I remember she always used to like to hang her pictures everywhere."

"They *were* full of Marina's pictures. She'd become an excellent photographer." Sam chose his words carefully. "Your mother's had a hard time dealing with her death. I came back one day to find she'd taken everything down. She said she couldn't bear to look at the wasted potential of her talent. That's partly why I suggested they move up-stairs. No memories there because Jake and Marina just had it renovated."

"But Mom removed other stuff, didn't she?" Kelly's pointed look made Sam realize there was no point in prevaricating. Her next words confirmed that. "I noticed the living room has discolored paint where I'm guessing a family or wedding picture used to hang." Her lips tightened. "She shouldn't have touched them. I'll ask her not to do it anymore."

"I've already told her not to," he admitted.

"Really?" Kelly stared at him. "You told my mother—" She stopped, a dazed look stretching her eyes wide.

"I had to. I want her to feel comfortable here, but I also want this to remain the kids' home," Sam explained. "Too many changes all at once aren't good for them. Your mother disagrees. She thinks they should forget as fast as they can."

"It's what she did with her own parents' deaths when we were little. We couldn't talk about our grandparents at all, though we had some very good memories." Kelly's sad face made Sam want to reassure her just as she'd reassured the twins. "That's how she deals with life's problems. Or at least it was when I lived at home."

"Maybe she'll get better," he soothed, doubting it.

"Thank you for understanding." Kelly's smile made it clear she knew he was soft-pedaling her mother's indignant reaction. "I'm sure she hasn't made it easy for you. I'm surprised she didn't push to have the funerals before I arrived."

"We need your input," was all he would admit. He smiled. "I was hoping you'd agree we should have them at their church, the one I showed you in town, and fairly soon. We all need the chance to say goodbye." He touched her arm, hating to cause her pain, but knowing it was inevitable. "I'd like to have one funeral for both of them on Saturday. Is that okay with you?"

"That's only two days away." He saw the tears well, but Kelly gulped, lifted her chin and nodded. "What do you need me to do?"

"Exactly what you just did, which is to take care of the kids. Listen to them when they want to talk. Comfort them, reassure them that they are loved and cared for." He had to say it. "I don't want Sadie and Emma to hear one word from anyone about not staying here on the ranch."

"Why aren't me and Emma stayin' here, Uncle Sam? Don't you want us no more?"

Sam wheeled around with a silent groan. Sadie stood in the doorway, her face drawn up in a frown.

"You're gonna send us away, aren't you, Uncle Sam?" she asked and then began to howl as if she was seriously injured.

Sam looked at Kelly and silently begged, *Help me!*

Kelly recognized grief, weariness and sadness in Sam's silent appeal. Poor guy was swamped with trying to keep the world going for everyone, including her. Kelly had to act. She scooped Sadie into her arms, set her on the bed then sat down beside her.

"Hush now. I want to ask you something, Sadie."

"'Kay," was the hiccupped response.

"Do you know Uncle Sam very well?" Kelly asked.

"O' course. He's Daddy's brother." Sadie frowned at the obviousness of that, but at least she'd stopped crying, and now her blue eyes widened with curiosity.

"Yes, but is Uncle Sam mean?" Kelly waited for Sadie to shake her head. "Does he do bad things?" Again the shake. "But I guess he sometimes yells at you."

"No. Uncle Sam loves me and Emma," Sadie insisted.

"Then why would he send you away from your home?" Kelly waited for her to puzzle it out. "Uncle Sam wouldn't do that, right?" Sadie shook her head. "Of course not. But you heard us talking and wondered why he said what he did."

"Uh-huh." Sadie's pigtails bobbed with her nod.

"Well, honey, it's like this. People are curious and sometimes they say silly things. I think Uncle Sam must have heard some of those folks talking, wondering about you and Emma."

"'Bout our mommy and daddy going away, you mean?" she said calmly, leaving Kelly to marvel at the quickness of this child's brain. "I think they said it 'cause Uncle Sam hasn't got a mommy."

"But—oh, you mean he doesn't have a wife who could care for you?" Kelly clarified.

"Uh-huh." Sadie frowned. "Who's gonna look after Emma 'n me?"

"Uncle Sam's going to look after you, honey. And I'm going to help him. If anyone asks you, you tell them that." She hugged Sadie close, somewhat surprised by how quickly love for these precious children had swept into her heart, a determined and protective love that refused to let Marina's beloved kids suffer unnecessarily.

"Okay now, darlin'?" Sam drawled as he crouched in front of Sadie.

"I guess." Her freckled nose wrinkled. "But who's my fam'ly?"

"Darlin', you got family coming out your ears." Sam tickled her earlobe then began listing people. "You have two grandmas, two grandpas, Uncle Sam, Auntie Kelly, Emma, Jacob Samuel and Oscar—"

"Oscar's my fam'ly?" Sadie's eyes peered at him in surprise.

"Oscar's our right-hand man," Sam explained to Kelly. He handed her the baby before turning back to Sadie to cup her cheeks in his palms. "He lives on the Triple D, doesn't he?" He grinned when she nodded. "Well then, Oscar must be family. Right, Kel?" he asked, holding her gaze with his own.

Kel. The nickname he'd given her the night of the wedding. Sam was the only one who'd ever called her that. Kelly couldn't help a thrill of pleasure at the familiarity. It made her feel part of the group, as though she belonged. Not even the memory of her mother's frosty reception could ruin the burst of warmth that sprang up inside.

Dear Sam. How kind of him to make her feel so welcome. Of course she was going to stay and help him, for as long as she could.

"Kel?" He was still watching her with that intent stare that saw too much.

"Right, Sam," she agreed, snapping out of her reverie. "Oscar must be family."

"See, Sadie Lady? What did I say?" He chuckled at Sadie's surprised look, but his attention returned to her. "Auntie Kel knows who's family."

His gaze held, probing, reassuring, warm. It felt as if Sam saw deep inside her to the secret childhood yearning to be loved unconditionally that had never quite gone away.

"Do ranch people eat dinner?" Kelly blurted, shifting under his stare. She rose, careful not to jostle Jacob Samuel, who was now sleeping. "I'm starving."

"It's not dinnertime yet," Sadie chided. "First Uncle Sam has to do chores."

"Tonight Oscar's going to do my chores," Sam explained as he took her hand on one side and Kelly's free one on the other then drew them both beside him toward the kitchen. "Kelly and I were rushing so hard to get here we only had a bit of breakfast and we missed lunch. I'm starving. Let's get a snack."

"Me an' Emma could make you our shake-'em-up pudding," Sadie volunteered as she swung his arm.

"Would you do that for us, darlin'?" Sam asked in a voice so tender, Kelly was nearly moved to tears. "I'd sure appreciate that. Wouldn't you, Kelly?"

"Shake-'em-up pudding sounds just right to me," she

agreed. "Only I don't know what it is. Can you show me how to make it, Sadie?"

"Sure." The little girl turned and bellowed, "Emma! Come an' help me. We gotta cook. Uncle Sam and Auntie Kel are hun-gry."

Sam barely smothered his laughter and winked at Kelly, who faked a cough to hide her own mirth. When Sadie frowned at her, Kelly made a big deal of pretending to regain her breath until the child finally turned away.

"Thanks." Sam's breath brushed her ear.

"That's why I'm here." Kelly smiled at him, enjoying the cozy feeling that being part of Sam's team brought. Until she caught a glimpse of her mother's face over Sam's shoulder.

"So that's how you think it will be, is it?" Arabella was clearly furious.

"Mom? What's wrong?" Kelly frowned when Arabella snatched Jacob Samuel from her arms, waking the little guy, who howled angrily at the disturbance.

"You've never bothered to make connections, to be there when you're needed, but now you think you'll waltz in here and take your sister's place, in her home—"

"What?" Stunned, Kelly stared at her, unable to believe she was hearing this. But Sam was not frozen by Arabella's bitter, angry words.

"Stop it," he ordered sternly. In one fluid move, he lifted Jacob from Arabella's startled grasp and handed the child back to Kelly before gripping Arabella's arm and firmly drawing her from the room, speaking over her angry protest. "I need to talk to you. Privately."

"Grannybell's mad," Sadie stated when they'd left. "You're in big trouble." She shook her head at Kelly then turned to order her sister to pour milk into a bowl.

Big trouble? Kelly stared into Jacob's scowling face and

jiggled him just in time to stop a yowl of anger or making strange or whatever he was doing.

"You're right, Sadie," she muttered with a sigh. "Almost ten years' worth of trouble. I guess the time's come to pay the piper."

"We don't have a piper." Sadie gave her a long look of pure pity before she turned back to her task, knocking over the milk jug as she did. Fortunately, Emma caught it. Sadie regally thanked her twin then returned to directing the pudding making.

A snicker from the doorway drew Kelly's attention. Sam stood just out of the kids' view, shoulders shaking with laughter. Kelly gave him a severe look. That was when she realized Jacob's diaper had leaked onto her shirt.

No piper to pay? Wanna make a bet?

As Sam tucked Jacob Samuel into his crib, he tried to remember the last time his sides had ached simply from laughing so hard. For a few moments he was overwhelmed by a pang of guilt. How could he laugh when his brother would never laugh again? But Jake and Marina would want their family to be happy. He'd have to keep reminding himself of that and of his Godsend, as his mother would put it, in finding Kelly.

Kelly had asked him what he'd said to her mother earlier, and so far Sam had managed to put her off by saying the matter was handled, but he knew perfectly well that Arabella would cause more trouble. She seemed very angry at her daughter, and Sam wasn't sure exactly why that was.

Fortunately, Kelly and his mom, Verna, had hit it off immediately when his parents had arrived a few hours earlier. While Arabella, claiming a migraine, stayed in her room, leaving Kelly's father, Neil, with Sam and the kids, Kelly and his mom had prepared a meal with the twins' pudding for dessert. They all worked hard to keep the atmosphere light when Kelly's mother finally came to the table. Jock Denver was a born peacemaker, and Sam could have hugged his dad when he drew Neil and Arabella into a conversation about downsizing.

While the men cleaned the dishes, Kelly helped Verna bathe the children under her mother's disapproving stare. Then Kelly snuggled in a chair with the twins for a bedtime tale about a princess who traveled on a big boat to faraway places. Enthralled by her soft voice and her descriptions of the same sights Sam had longed for years to see, the twins begged Kelly to keep going when she said it was bedtime. She assured them that installments would follow each night if they didn't fuss about going to bed.

Sam guessed Kelly was making the tale up as she went, drawing from her own travels to bring the story to life, and he was at least as curious about the next chapter as Sadie and Emma.

"Auntie Kel said bedtime," he reminded softly when Sadie began to argue. He wanted to scoop her in his arms and assure her they'd have tomorrow, and tomorrow after that. But he couldn't do that because he wasn't sure how long Kelly would stay. Sadie gave him a mutinous look, but Sam didn't budge. "Bedtime."

"Okay." With a huge sigh Sadie slid off the sofa, grabbed Emma's hand and walked with her down the hall to their room. After a glance at him, Kelly followed.

Sam went, too, his heart tight in his chest at what was to come. Emma and Sadie knelt by their beds. Since Sam had already put Jacob Samuel down, he had no excuse when Sadie patted the top of her bed, indicating he should sit there. He felt Kelly watching, waiting for his lead. Swallowing his discomfort at this brush with God, Sam sat down on Sadie's bed while Kelly sat on Emma's.

"We gotta pray now," Emma told her aunt in her whisper-quiet voice.

Kelly obediently bowed her head and closed her eyes. A swath of dark hair flopped down to caress each molded cheekbone. When his bossy niece cleared her throat, Sam reluctantly stopped staring at his beautiful sister-in-law, bowed his own head and closed his eyes.

"Hi, God. It's me, Sadie. Thanks for bringing our aunt Kelly here. We like her lots. And Uncle Sam is the best-est." Sadie sighed. Surprised by her silence, Sam opened his eyes. Sadie's face was scrunched up in thought. "I sure do wish You didn't take my mommy and daddy away, though. Will You tell them I'm trying to be good? It's hard." She paused as if she wasn't sure how to continue.

Sam was about to intervene when Emma urged, "Say the God-blesses, Sadie."

"I know how to pray." Sadie glared at her sister then caught Sam with his eyes open, watching Kelly. She frowned, waited till he'd closed them again then continued. "God bless Gran and Grandpa, Grannybell and Grandpa Neil, Jacob Samuel and Uncle Sam and Auntie Kelly. And Emma," she added as if it was an afterthought. "And God bless me. Amen."

Emma's prayer was much shorter but just as heartfelt, though barely audible. Sam wasn't even certain she'd said amen until Kelly rose.

"I love you, Sadie Lady." He bent and hugged the little girl, inhaling the soft fragrance of her shampoo. His heart stopped for a minute when she squeezed her arms around his neck and held on tight, as if she was afraid to let go in case he disappeared. "Sleep tight, darlin'." He kissed her forehead.

"Love you, Uncle Sam," she murmured on the back side of a yawn and let go.

"Good night, Emma, my gem." The child's frequent si-lences worried him, but for now Sam stuffed that away to give her an extralong hug. "I love you, sweetheart. Sleep well."

"G'night, Uncle Sam," she breathed.

He waited at the door while Kelly said her good-nights, noting the affection in her voice and how her brown eyes softened as she touched each girl's cheek with her lips. His heart breathed a sigh of relief that the three had bonded so quickly. If only he could persuade Kelly to stick around...

With one last good-night, Sam flicked on a night-light, ushered Kelly into the hallway and eased the door almost closed. He followed Kelly to the empty living room and sat opposite her in his brother's recliner, glad that both their parents had gone elsewhere. He was too tired to play mediator tonight.

"You're worried about something, Sam." Kelly studied him with a grave look marring her lovely face. "Can I help?"

"I'm concerned about Emma," he confessed, liking that she cared enough to ask.

"She's a very quiet child," Kelly agreed thoughtfully.

"Too quiet. She wasn't always, though. It's only since Marina and Jake died that she's started this—I don't know what to call it. Whispering?" He rubbed the cord in his neck that was painfully tight. "I have a hunch it has to do with something she's worried about but since—well, lately she hasn't been confiding like she used to." He had a sudden thought. "You've already built a rapport with the girls. Maybe you could find out."

"You think Emma will confide in me, a stranger, when she doesn't tell you or her grandparents what's bothering her?" Kelly's face revealed her skepticism.

"You and Marina were twins. Jake and I were, too." Sam remembered times when Jake had dashed into something when Sam himself would have thought about it more carefully before acting. "You and I know there's usually one twin who's more dominant."

"And that's Sadie, obviously." Kelly frowned. "Are you suggesting that if I spent some time with Emma away from Sadie, she might talk?" He nodded. "I can give it a try."

"Thanks." Sam couldn't shake the question hanging in the air so he faced it head-on. "What's the deal between you and your mother?" From the way Kelly flushed and avoided his gaze, he knew she didn't want to discuss it.

"I'm so sorry you had to witness that." Shame colored her voice, showed in the slump of her shoulders. "I guess she's still angry with me."

"Why?" Sam waited, wondering at the myriad emotions that stormed across Kelly's face. "You can tell me, Kelly. I won't judge. But I won't pry, either."

"Actually, I don't want to talk about it," she murmured, avoiding his gaze. "Suffice it to say I was never the daughter she wanted."

"What's that mean?" Confused by her words, Sam wanted to know more, but the pain on Kelly's face told him that whatever had happened so long ago still hurt her.

"My mother has some strict beliefs about parenting and especially obedience." Kelly summoned a smile but there was no mirth in it. "Marina managed to heed her orders, but I always wanted to know why." She made a face. "I guess I'm a late bloomer, because it's only lately that I've begun to accept that I can't always know the *why* of things."

"Actually, you and Marina sound a lot like Sadie and Emma." Sam smiled at her surprise.

"I guess we were." Kelly sighed. "You have to know that I loved my sister very much. She was everything I wanted to be. Only I couldn't be her, and that caused problems so I stayed away."

Sam heard a finality in that response, so he didn't press for answers. There would be time for that later. Instead, he asked a question he'd carried for almost ten years. "How did you happen to fall for my brother?"

Kelly's head jerked up. She gaped at him. "You knew?"

"Those puppy-dog looks you shot his way when you thought I wasn't looking sort of gave it away. To me," he added on seeing her worried look. "If it makes you feel better, I doubt anyone else guessed you loved Jake back then."

Odd, Sam thought, how that old tickle of envy for his brother's easy draw of females ruffled his feelings even now, and he barely knew Kelly, especially after ten years.

"Jake was a friend when I really needed one." Kelly's smile chased away the sorrow that lingered and emphasized her loveliness. Sam's heart gave a bump of admiration that he quickly stifled. "We were both young, away from home for the first time and mixed up about our faith. We were in the same classes at Bible school, and we helped each other sort out what we believed. We had fun together."

"And you fell in love with him," Sam reminded.

"Yes. Or I persuaded myself that I did."

Why did Kelly's words send a flush of relief through him? Sam didn't pause to examine that now. "So you didn't love Jake?"

"I don't know. I'd never been in love before." Kelly's forehead furrowed as she thought over her answer. "My mother was pushing me hard to become a missionary, and Jake helped me see that giving in to her wasn't necessarily what God wanted for me." She shot him a rueful smile. "Sometimes I think Jake's major attraction back then was that I believed he'd help me escape those arguments with my mom."

"Instead, he fell for your sister." Relieved to note Kelly's simple nod, Sam decided she didn't seem to be nursing any lingering feelings. "So if you weren't still mooning over Jake, why not come back earlier?"

"I can't talk about it now." Her voice tightened as she

said, "All I can say is that I stayed away because that's what my mother wanted." Her eyes suddenly welled with tears. "But Marina was my sister. I had to come now."

"Of course you did," Sam soothed, deeply moved by her distress. "I'm glad you're here, Kelly. We need you here. All of us."

"You're a really nice man, Sam. Thank you for saying that." She dashed away the tears. "I'll try to help however I can. I want to ensure Marina's kids end up with you as their father."

"But you hardly know me," he protested, though flattered by her words.

"I think I know you very well." Kelly studied him, a faint smile tugging at her mobile lips. "Working on a cruise ship, you learn to sum up people pretty quickly. I can see you'll be an amazing father. It's obvious you love the kids, so I know your concern will be for them first, last and always."

"How do you know that?" Sam asked curiously, though pleased by her flattering assessment.

"It's there for anyone to see in everything you do with them," Kelly said. "You've sensed that Emma isn't herself so you're trying to figure out what's troubling her. I've watched you give Jacob Samuel extra cosseting when he's fussing, seen you rein in headstrong Sadie in a gentle but firm way." She leaned forward, utterly serious. "You don't see their individual traits as problems but as wonderful parts of their personality to be enhanced and explored. You are their father now, Sam, in every way that counts."

"Thank you." Sam's throat jammed at her generous words.

"This is where you belong, caring for them," Kelly said. "But I don't. I'll stay for six months. Then I have to go."

"Have to?" he asked softly.

"Yes." She sounded sad. "You have the ranch, your parents, the kids. They're an integral part of your world. They define you."

"What defines you?" he asked.

"My career. Without that, I have nothing." Kelly rose regally, like the princess in her story.

Sam's heart ached for her as she walked toward the door, a solitary figure. She stopped there and turned around.

"Until I leave, I'll do everything I can to help you. You only have to ask." Her brown eyes narrowed, held him. "I have just one request."

"Name it." Sam would have promised anything, that was how relieved he was that Kelly was staying. At least for now.

"Don't tell my mother I intend to leave. Not yet. Let her think I'm here for good." A painful smile barely lifted Kelly's wide mouth. "Maybe over the next few months she'll begin to see who I am." Her voice dropped to a whisper. "Don't let her control you, Sam. I couldn't bear for her to make Sadie as unhappy as I once was."

Kelly left, her tread soundless down the hallway. Sam mulled over the little bit she'd told him and realized that all he'd learned was that there was a vast chasm between mother and daughter. For the next six months he would accept whatever help Kelly offered. But he was also going to try to help her rebuild her relationship with her mom. Maybe if he did that, maybe if he could make her feel she was a necessary and integral part of this new family they were forging, then she wouldn't want to leave. Maybe Kelly would make a new life here.

It seemed important to help Kelly, though Sam was doing it for the kids' sake. He liked his sister-in-law and wanted her to be happy. She was also one of the most beautiful women he'd ever known. He enjoyed having someone his age to talk to and share his world. Yet he could picture

Kelly in twenty years, still here on the ranch. Of course, that could be just his lonely imagination.

Kelly would make a wonderful mother for the kids. But she could never be more than his sister-in-law because Sam wasn't going to let romance into his life again. He wasn't going to make himself that vulnerable, and he sure wasn't going to give God another chance to ignore him.

In truth, Sam's dream of sharing the future with a woman was as dead as his dream of travel. But he could be, would be, a father to Jake's kids. To do that, he'd take every bit of help Kelly offered.

Chapter Three

It seemed the entire town of Buffalo Gap turned out for the joint funeral of Marina and Jake Denver. For Kelly, busy preparing the kids and answering their many questions, the full impact of this final goodbye finally hit on Saturday afternoon as she sat in a pew next to Sam, listening to Pastor Don speak of the couple with love.

"We can't wish them back, though we miss them terribly," he said. "They're in a much better place, with their heavenly Father, at peace in His presence. We must trust Him to help us look past our own grief to help the family they've left behind. The children Jake and Marina loved so much will need us to be there, to listen, to comfort and to support. So will their families. It's time to show our love, people."

There was more, but the rest of the words flew over Kelly's head as her gaze meshed with Sam's. He looked utterly bereft, so terribly sad that it hurt to look at him. She had to do something. Kelly slipped her hand into his and squeezed. He turned his head and studied her for a long moment before he returned the squeeze. A very faint smile tilted his lips before his attention slid to the front of the church and settled on the large photo of Jake and Marina laughing at some shared joke. Sam had told her this morning that he'd taken that picture, snapped it the day Marina had learned she was pregnant with Jacob Samuel.

Oh, Marina.

Emotions of all descriptions tore through Kelly; loss, grief, guilt, pain—but most of all a question. Why? She wanted so badly to understand why God had chosen this way and yet, hadn't she learned not to question His will? She kept her head bowed to hide her expression from the kids until Sam's fingers, still holding hers, returned the squeeze a second time. He leaned toward her.

"She's happy," he murmured in her ear. "We have to remember that."

Kelly nodded, surprised by how easily his soft words and gentle touch soothed her sore heart. Finally, the service was over. They filed out of the church and into limos that took them to the graveyard. Kelly heard her mother's sobs but kept her focus on the kids, watching for signs that she was needed, stuffing down the grief that waited to overwhelm her.

She and Sam had carefully explained every step to the twins, who stood clinging to each other, silenced by the somber occasion, though their big blue eyes took in every detail. Jacob Samuel slept quietly in his uncle's arms, his thumb shoved between his lips.

Once everyone was gathered in the graveyard with the chilly wind tugging at their garments, Pastor Don spoke about the resurrection when they would see Jake and Marina again. After a gentle prayer, the matching caskets were lowered into the cold ground.

"Ashes to ashes…" The familiar words took on new meaning as Pastor Don tossed a handful of dirt over the caskets and then led them in reciting the Lord's Prayer. Then it was over, the sad celebration for two vibrant lives.

It was over but Kelly couldn't move. Time seemed to freeze. It isn't enough, she wanted to yell. There should be something more to leave the mark of two wonderful people. But she couldn't dwell on that. Her job was to ensure the twins were all right. She glanced sideways at the two small girls who, hand in hand, stepped to the edge of the grave. They hadn't discussed this. Kelly glanced at Sam, knew he was about to restrain them until Sadie spoke.

"Bye, Mommy and Daddy. We love you."

Emma simply whispered, "Bye." Then after a moment she added, "We'll look after Jacob Samuel."

Kelly could no more have stopped her tears than stopped breathing. A quick check told her Sam's eyes were also moist. He handed Jacob Samuel to his mother then drew Kelly with him to stand beside the girls. Then he hunkered down and wrapped an arm around each of them.

"I'm very proud of you two," he said, his voice cracked and broken with love. "I love you very much. I always will."

"We love you, too, Uncle Sam." Sadie, always the most verbal, kissed him on one cheek, and Emma kissed him on the other before drawing Kelly into their circle.

"Sadie says you're going to be our mommy and daddy now." Emma's whisper barely penetrated the hushed conversations of friends and neighbors around the gravesite. "She said we're still a family. Is that right?"

Kelly didn't know what to say. How could she give them hope when they didn't know what was going to happen with the adoptions? But Sam had no such compunction.

"Auntie Kel and I are going to look after you the very best we can," he assured them. "Don't you worry about that." He rose, his big strong hands around the girls' tiny ones. "We're going to go back to the church now."

"For lunch." Sadie nodded wisely. "I hope they have cupcakes. I love cupcakes."

"Me, too." Emma slipped her free hand into Kelly's. "But I love Mommy and Daddy better," she murmured in a sad, forlorn voice that brought a lump to Kelly's throat.

"Me, too, Emma," was all she could say.

The girls sat uncharacteristically silent on the ride back to the church. Once there, their grandparents took charge of them while Sam's friends and neighbors offered their condolences and help with whatever he needed. He thanked them then scrupulously introduced Kelly. The names blurred in Kelly's brain. Until he introduced Abby Lebret.

"You're the woman from the adoption agency," Kelly remembered. "Family Ties, right? You found the twins for Marina and Jake." It hurt to say her name, knowing her sister was forever gone.

"That's me." Abby smiled as she introduced her husband, Cade, then her face sobered. "Not now but sometime soon I need to talk to both of you."

"That sounds ominous," Sam said. When Abby didn't respond, he added, "Can you come over later today?"

"We can wait a day, Sam," Abby protested. "It's not that urgent."

"I want—" He gave Kelly a sideways look and began again. "Kelly and I want to get things settled with the twins as soon as possible, for their sakes." His face took on a grim look. "They need to feel secure."

"I agree." Abby finally nodded. "Okay. I'll come out to the Triple D later this afternoon."

"Thank you." Sam nodded. When Abby and her husband had moved on, he turned to Kelly. "I don't like the sound of that. Something's going on."

"What?" she asked.

"Beats me, but Abby wouldn't ask for a meeting if there wasn't a good reason." He turned away to accept sympathy from someone else, leaving Kelly to stew about the upcoming get-together. Since her mother was now supervising the twins at the lunch table, she slipped away, wandering from the fellowship room into the sanctuary of the church, where she sat down in a window nook.

She'd thought this trip would be a simple matter of helping Sam get things settled, figuring out a care schedule for the kids, something of that nature. But everything was becoming more complicated, and that included her reactions to the big, handsome rancher.

I'm beginning to rely on him, to seek his opinion. She grimaced. *It's not what I'm used to.*

These past nine years, she'd made her own decisions based on proving herself by rising to the top of her field. Now suddenly it seemed she couldn't decide anything without considering how it would affect the kids, her parents, the ranch and especially without hearing Sam's opinion.

The trouble was, she liked Sam. He was earnest, trustworthy, a guy who put others first. He wasn't afraid to show his emotions as were so many men. He didn't bolt when hard problems came up. He searched for a solution that would benefit everyone. Kelly found that so admirable. In fact, Sam was as close to a hero as she'd ever met.

But this confusing soft spot for him couldn't blossom into anything else. She wasn't here for romance. For a long time she'd prayed for a family, a husband, a home of her own. God hadn't answered that prayer. Just because she felt welcome here, was needed for a little while, didn't mean anything had changed. Her mother was right. Kelly could not step into the middle of Marina's family and take over.

Not that she wanted to, she reminded herself. There were so many places she had yet to explore, so many things to discover. For three years she'd dreamed of visiting Indonesia. Okay, that had to be put on hold, but the goal hadn't faded. She still wanted to go there.

As much as you want to see Sadie and Emma grow up?

I can't support myself here, she told that contrary voice in her head. *The only job I know is cruising. It's what I do. It's what I'm good at, even if Mom doesn't think it worthy of her daughter.*

Which meant that come August, once Sam and the kids were settled, Kelly would return to her life on the seas. She'd trod a hard path to learn that was God's plan for her, and having done so, she was committed to following God's will no matter what the personal cost.

"Face it, kiddo. This is only a temporary stop on your life's path," she whispered. "Be a blessing however you can so that when it's time to go, you leave with no regrets."

But even as she said it, Kelly had a hunch that when she finally left the Triple D, saying goodbye to Sam would be difficult.

Sam glanced around the fellowship hall, worried when he was unable to spot Kelly's slim figure among the few friends still left in the room. Neither his parents nor hers knew where she'd gone. Sadie and Emma were in a corner playing with their dolls. He walked over and crouched down beside them.

"Did you two see where Auntie Kel went?" he asked, not really expecting an answer.

"Into the church," Sadie said.

"She's sad," Emma whispered.

"*In* the church?" He frowned. "But we're already in the—oh." Realizing they meant the sanctuary, he made sure they were under supervision then rose to search out Kelly. It took a minute to spy her seated in the dim light. When he did, the tears streaming down her face made him swallow, hard. "Kelly, what's wrong?"

"This is where Marina prayed, Sam. She brought her kids here to learn about God. She came here to gather with her friends to share her dreams." She gulped then lifted her heavily lashed lids to gaze at him, eyes shiny. "I can't seem to accept that I won't ever be able to hear those dreams or tell her mine, or find out what she loved most about living on the ranch. I can't tell my sister how sorry I am I didn't come earlier." She wept as if her heart was breaking.

"She knew." Sam drew her into his arms, holding her as he tried to comfort her with the only words he had. "Sisters, brothers, twins—we all have an intangible bond, Kelly. We know we're loved, even if we don't get around to saying it to each other often enough." He smoothed a hand down her back, hoping his words would offer her a bit of ease. "Marina knew you cared about her."

"Did she?" She took the handkerchief he offered and dabbed at her eyes.

"I know it. And deep inside, I think you do, too." Even red-eyed and weeping, Kelly was a stunning woman. As she drew away, Sam's arms felt bereft. For a moment he recalled the companionship and affection he'd found with Naomi. Then he remembered that God had let her die, and the lump of hurt inside him that had begun to soften solidified once more.

"I'm sorry to weep all over you." Kelly forced a smile to her pretty lips. "I guess I needed a moment to regroup."

"Nothing wrong with that. I should have made sure you had some free time earlier," he apologized ruefully. He'd been so worried about the kids he hadn't given a thought to Kelly's grief. Was that because he didn't want to think about his own loss and the emptiness of his life without Jake?

"How do you handle it, Sam?" Kelly stared at him curiously. "Do you question God?"

"About many things," he said with a dredged-up smile. "I'm trying to accept that even though I don't like it, it was time for Marina and Jake to go." He hesitated then spoke what lay on his heart. "At least God didn't let them linger and suffer first."

"He did that with someone else?" Kelly's soft voice soothed like a cool palm on a thudding forehead. "Someone you loved."

That part was not a question, but Sam nodded anyway.

"Naomi?" It wasn't sheer nosiness that made Kelly ask. He could tell from her body language, the angle of her head and the way she leaned forward, that she was searching for something to help ease her own bereavement.

"My fiancée." Sam swallowed. It had been a long time since he'd discussed this with anyone, including Jake. "She got cancer."

Kelly waited, hands folded in her lap, watching him. He stared at the picture of the Good Shepherd. Jesus cradled a small lamb in one arm. His eyes oozed kindness and understanding, but Sam wouldn't let himself be swayed by the lure of faith because he couldn't survive being let down by God again.

He felt her warm fingers curl around his, nudging away the lingering sadness. "I'm so sorry, Sam."

"So am I. She was a great person, served God with everything she had. Nothing was too much for Naomi if it was for her Lord." He rose, paced in front of Kelly as all the old questions bubbled up once more. "She was His child," Sam blurted, unable to harness the anger roiling inside. "Why make her suffer?"

"I don't know."

Though embarrassed by his outburst, Sam liked that Kelly didn't make excuses or offer a silly reason like "for the greater good." Neither did Kelly trot out the familiar adages that God is always good or that He always does what's best for His children. She was the only person he'd spoken to about Naomi's death who didn't try to make him the bad guy for questioning God.

"I wish I had answers for you, Sam." Kelly rose, smoothed her clothes then looked directly at him. "I get through the days by hanging on to one thing. God understands what I'm feeling because He suffered, too. His son was murdered so He knows all about grief." Her voice dropped almost to a whisper. "I'm sorry you're suffering."

"Thanks." Why was he crying on her shoulder instead of trying to comfort her? Sam shook his head to disperse the past. "I wish you didn't have to leave," he admitted quietly.

"More time wouldn't help." Her lovely mouth lifted in the beginning of a smile. "Anyway, I have six months to do whatever I can to help you adopt the twins. But then I have to go back where I belong."

"You belong here with your family," he protested, intrinsically knowing it was true.

"I don't have a place in your family, Sam. I don't even have one in mine." Her voice wobbled slightly, but she got it under control with a halfhearted chuckle. "I belong on a cruise ship."

"That's not true. Your father—"

"Soon won't notice if I'm here or not," she finished, her voice sad. "This morning he forgot my name. That's not going to improve, so I'll just have to make the most of the time we have together." She inclined her head. "We'd better get back to the others."

"Yes. I've left the twins too long," he agreed with a wry look. "Stay here if you need a few more moments alone."

"I don't." She gave him a spunky grin. "But even if I did, I'm too afraid of what we'll find if we don't get back to the twins now."

"You're learning." Sam chuckled as he walked with her to the fellowship room. Sure enough, Sadie stood toe-to-toe with Arabella.

"*No*, you can't say that about Auntie Kelly," she told her grandmother in an iron voice. Sadie turned her back, took Emma's hand and led her toward Sam. "We're going home. Now."

"Yes, we are," he agreed, thankful that the room was empty except for the two sets of grandparents, the pastor and some of the church ladies who'd served the food. "You two get your coats on but stay inside. We'll go home in one of the big white cars." He shot Kelly a look, hoping she'd recognize his silent request for help.

"I'll come with you, girls," she said immediately. "Uncle Sam, do you think they'll warm up the car while we're getting ready?"

"Yes, ma'am." He leaned down near her ear to tease, "West Coast weakling. Can't take a little cold?"

"It's not a *little* cold." Kelly leaned back to inform him in a pert tone, eyes sparkling with challenge. "It's an Arctic blast, and I can hardly wait to get out of it."

"You can't leave us, Auntie Kel!" Sadie grabbed her hand and clung. "Please? I'll be good. I won't yell at Grannybell anymore, even if she does say bad things."

"Bad things like what?" Sam immediately demanded with a frown at Arabella.

Sadie risked a look over one shoulder before she answered in the quietest voice Sam had ever heard her use.

"She said Auntie Kelly is going away because she never stays anywhere, and that Aunt Abby is gonna get us a new mommy and daddy. She said Emma and me might have to live in different houses."

With steely control, Sam swallowed his anger. This was the house of God, a place Jake and Marina had taught the girls to revere. He wasn't about to set a bad example, but he *was* going to straighten out Arabella and now was as good a time as any.

"That's not right, Sadie." Sam hunkered down to her level, unable to help himself from issuing a heartfelt prayer that God wouldn't make him wrong about this. "Your home is on the ranch with me, Sadie Lady. You and Emma are my family. Aunt Abby's going to help us make sure it stays that way. Okay?"

"Sure?" Sadie studied his face, eyes trusting. "Certain

sure?" It was their special code, a cross-your-heart kind of promise that Sam wouldn't break his word.

Please don't let me disappoint her, God. Prayer number two—from a man who no longer prayed?

"Certain sure," he insisted, too aware of Kelly watching him with a warning in her dark gaze. Sam ignored it as Sadie threw herself into his arms. He hugged her close, closed his eyes and inhaled that special fragrance that could only be Sadie while he mustered his third plea.

Just this once could You answer my prayer?

Chapter Four

Kelly had no idea what Sam said to her mother, but later that afternoon a chastened Arabella declined the offer to join the family for dinner, claiming a headache. She even declined the tray Kelly brought to her.

"I just want to sleep, to forget this day ever happened," she said tearfully. "I want my daughter back." Then her voice hardened as her shoulders went back. "I should never have allowed Marina to come to this place."

"Allowed her?" Kelly gaped at her mother. "Mom, you couldn't have stopped her. Marina loved it here with Jake and the kids. This was her home. She *chose* to live here and it *was* her choice."

"You don't understand." Arabella's scathing tone hurt, but Kelly kept her focus.

"You think not?" She couldn't quite rid her voice of sarcasm. "Marina was my sister, my *twin* sister. I feel her loss as deeply as you, but I can't wish her back. Why would I when she's with her Lord?"

"You don't understand because you haven't had children. A mother feels things differently when it's her own child. There's a connection that's like no other connection." Arabella sniffed.

"The same might be said about twins," Kelly murmured,

trying not to feel hurt that her mother apparently found no such connection with her.

"Those twins would be better off somewhere else." Arabella's lips clamped together in a tight line.

"How can you say that?" Aghast, Kelly stared at the woman she'd never felt she understood. "*This* is their home."

"Their foster home. Temporary. They'll make a new home with some other woman." Arabella shrugged. "Marina wasn't their real mother no matter how much everyone pretends."

"She was as much their mother as she was Jacob Samuel's." Kelly grit her teeth when Arabella shook her head.

"The connection between mother and child comes from carrying a baby near your heart for nine months. Marina had that with Jacob Samuel." Her face wan, Arabella leaned back against her pillow with a sigh. "But she made do with the twins."

"You mean like they were second best?" Indignant, Kelly smothered the words she longed to say to snap her mother back to reality. She was here to make things better, not worse. "If Marina heard you say that she'd be furious, Mom. She loved the twins as much as if they were her own flesh and blood. Pretending she didn't is not a credit to her memory."

"You're pretending, sidling up to Sam, acting as if her family is yours because you have no one in your life." There was a kind of sneering sound to the words. "Why did you come back, Kelly?" her mother demanded.

The question stopped Kelly in her tracks. She refused to show how deeply those words wounded. "I came back because my twin sister died, and I wanted to be here to help however I could."

"So once the twins are placed in another home, you'll leave." Her mother looked unbothered by that possibility.

"I'll be here until Sam doesn't need me." Kelly decided

to make it clear to her mother that she wasn't going to let the twins go without a fight. "I intend to help him ensure Sadie and Emma stay here with him on the ranch, where they belong."

"You know the adoptions didn't go through, so this is just a temporary home. They'll go and so will you because none of you belong here." Arabella nodded sagely then picked up a slice of the toast Kelly had brought and began nibbling at one corner.

Kelly fought tears, astounded by her words. Talk about unwanted.

"Technically, I guess you and Dad don't belong here, either, and yet Sam has graciously made you feel welcome while you deal with Dad's illness." She looked her mother straight in the eye, finally giving voice to the hurt that she'd kept buried for years. "You had two daughters and one of them is still alive, Mother. But it seems you feel as little for me as you do for Marina's twins. Thanks for the welcome home."

Kelly had expected to see emotion on her mother's face, maybe an expression of sorrow as she realized how her daughter felt, something. Instead, Arabella simply stared at her blankly. Kelly grasped the door handle, walked into the hall and carefully, soundlessly pulled the door closed behind her. Only then did she give in to silent weeping. What had she ever done that her own mother so easily disowned her?

"Kelly?" Sam stood on the top stair, his expression growing rueful when he glimpsed her wet face. He probably thought she was weeping for Marina. "I didn't mean to interrupt. I only came to tell you we're waiting supper for you." He stopped then asked in a soft voice, "Is everything all right?"

"I'm coming." She cleared her throat. "I had something in my eye, that's all. I think it's gone now." Dabbing away her tears, she forced a smile as she walked toward him. "My mother is fine."

That was a lie. Something was wrong with Arabella that wouldn't let her show love, and Kelly had no idea what it was. But in the days to come she was going to try to discover why, not for herself but because the twins would need the entire family's support for Sam to get custody.

Just before they entered the kitchen, where she could hear the twins chattering, Sam stopped her with a hand on her arm.

"After supper my mom said she and Dad will watch the kids here while you and I meet with Abby at my place. Okay?" he asked, one eyebrow arched.

"Sure." Kelly hated the rush of trepidation she felt. "Any idea what it's about?"

"Could be several things." Sam's gaze held hers. "But we'll handle it together, right?"

"For the next six months we're a team, Sam. We're going to get that adoption through. We can do it." Kelly infused her words with as much confidence as she could, knowing that upstairs lay a huge roadblock to that plan.

"Kelly and Sam. Who could resist them?" he joked. But his teasing tone couldn't mask the worry lurking at the back of his green gaze. "Nobody messes with our family."

Our family.

It sounded so good. Kelly held up her hand to receive his high five then preceded him into the kitchen. She took her place at the table with her father on one side and Jacob Samuel on the other. As Sam's father said grace, she found herself watching Sam, utterly bemused at his inclusion of her in his family. How wonderful to belong.

Even if it was only for six months.

"The twins' father had an aunt," Abby said quietly. "Whoever was in charge of finding their family after their mother died had no idea about her because she married and changed her name. Then she was divorced and has since remarried. She's been out of touch with the family for a long time."

"But why didn't their father mention this person?" Sam said, frustration eating at him. Why wasn't God doing something?

"I'm not sure. Apparently, this aunt divorced her husband when the twins' father was quite young. Perhaps he forgot about her," Abby offered. "Remember their father already has a family and has made it very clear he's disowned the twins and given up all his parental rights."

"Maybe he also disowned his aunt," Kelly suggested. Sam could tell from the way she'd said the words that she was still smarting from the contretemps with her mother that had left her weeping in the hall, though he wasn't sure exactly what had happened.

"Could be," Abby agreed. "Anyway, this woman, Eunice Edwards, recently took up a hobby—genealogy. While building her family tree, she learned of the existence of the twins. She and her second husband, Tom, are childless. They have petitioned the court for custody of the twins."

"Wait a minute. I thought of something." Kelly's brain was busy processing this new information as Sam felt a rush of devastation.

He appreciated that she was trying to find a fragment of hope, but he needed something more than a feeling to go on.

"This woman would be the twins' great-aunt, correct?" Kelly's brown eyes sparkled.

"Yes." Abby smiled at her. "I see our minds are moving along similar channels."

"What channels?" Sam glanced from her to Kelly. "What are you both thinking?"

"That a great-aunt would be older and maybe not as able to handle almost-five-year-old twins." Kelly studied

Abby's face then frowned. "Except you mentioned a husband. That family aspect probably gives her claim more credence than an uncle who is unmarried and isn't even legally an uncle. True?"

"In the court's eyes—likely," Abby agreed quietly.

"So what now?" Sam demanded, his jaw muscles flexing. "I'm supposed to just hand them over?"

"No. A judge will have to hear their claim," Abby explained. "You'll be able to present your side. We have Marina and Jake's documents showing that they'd prepared for their children's futures by naming guardians in the event that something happened to them. That shows responsibility. You also have a family network of support, Sam. That counts."

Despite her words, Sam didn't think she sounded optimistic.

"Uh, about family." Kelly cleared her throat. "Don't count on my mother for support, Abby. She thinks the twins should be sent to someone else."

"What?" So that was what Arabella had laid on Kelly. Sam watched a flush of shame fill her face and wished he'd been there to support her. "Why does she want them gone?"

"I can't figure that out." Kelly tried to smile. Sam thought it was to soften her next words. "My mother seems to feel Marina only accepted the twins as a kind of second-best substitute, that Jacob Samuel's birth, the birth of her own child," Kelly emphasized, "meant she didn't really want them anymore."

"That's a lie!" The startled look on both women's faces made him realize he'd shouted the words. Sam swallowed then explained in a quieter tone. "Marina adored the twins. She loved making their clothes, telling them stories, planning the future with them. She was constantly assuring them that she and Jake would never let them go."

"Sam—" Abby tried to interrupt, but he had to finish.

"There is nothing second-best in the videos she made to chronicle their lives over this past year," he insisted, smarting at the idea that his brother would have let his beloved twins go without a fight. "They loved Sadie and Emma every bit as much as they loved Jacob Samuel."

"Okay, good. The videos will be powerful evidence for our case, showing the twins are part of the family," Abby mused, but her face remained troubled. "The biggest hole in our case is that Kelly isn't staying. Sam said you intend to leave in six months?"

"I have to go back to work." Kelly's beseeching eyes begged them both to understand. "It's my job. I don't know how to do anything else, and I have to earn a living somehow."

"Oh, I realize that. It's just that the judge will be certain to ask who will be there to watch the kids, all three of them, when you're gone." Abby glanced from Kelly to Sam. "Any ideas how you'll handle that?"

"Not yet," he said, hearing the defensiveness in his voice. "But I'll come up with something. It's not an impossible situation. People have nannies."

"True," Abby conceded. "There are lots of single parents who have day care or other options. But this great-aunt has a large house, with servants, and intends to hire a full-time caregiver. She's already started the twins' college fund, too."

"A pity she didn't provide for them when their mother was alive," Kelly grumbled.

"If she had, Sadie and Emma might never have come here," Sam reminded her. "I can't wish that." He noticed Kelly's embarrassed look and reached out to pat her shoulder. "I like that you're angry on the twins' behalf, though."

"Mrs. Edwards claims she didn't know about her nephew's affair, that the woman had children or that she was ill. Now that she knows, she wants to give them a life of opportunity."

Abby sighed. "I only wanted you to be aware. There's nothing you can do at the moment, but I'd suggest that while we're waiting, you strengthen your case by ensuring the twins continue to think of this as home and you two as their caregivers."

"And my mom?" Kelly asked, her voice hesitant. "What do we do about her? She's living here. She'll unsettle them, undo what we're trying to do because she doesn't think the girls belong here."

"She isn't going home?" Abby asked.

"She can't." Shamefaced, Sam looked at Kelly. "She was really struggling with your dad. When I was there visiting, I kind of suggested she sell the house and move here so she could be near Marina and get help if she needed it. Apparently, Arabella took my advice, because I found out yesterday that she has accepted an offer on their house in Victoria. Their things are being packed and moved here as we speak."

"Mom never told me." Kelly stared at him as if he'd betrayed her. Sam hated that.

"She thinks she and your dad should stay with you in Marina and Jake's house," he confessed.

"No." Kelly shook her head adamantly. "I'm leaving in six months. Dad's condition is getting worse. I know he needs familiar things and places, but he also needs care. Caring for the kids, your parents and mine is asking too much of you, Sam. Besides, Mom's attitude toward the twins is controlling and very negative. My parents need their own place, nearby maybe, but separate."

"I have an idea. Mayor Marsha mentioned her sister and husband, who winter in Arizona, intend to move to the coast to be near their grandchildren." Abby shrugged. "Marsha said they were waiting till spring to list their house, but maybe something could be worked out."

Sam knew who she was talking about.

"Good idea. Even better, the Emersons' house is very

similar to your parents' home in Victoria," he told Kelly. "Put their own things in it, and I think your dad would settle. He's not at the total confusion stage yet and managed the move to the ranch very well. Waiting might make it harder for him." He watched Kelly process the information. "Would your mom consider it?"

"Maybe." She tilted her head. "You'd have to present it with no other option but moving because unless you do, she will insist on staying here. My mother likes to be in control."

"Understatement," Sam muttered. He saw Kelly's amusement and hurried to change the subject. "Problem is she's concerned about staying with your dad without help." Frustration returned, accompanied by irritation. Could God actually *want* the twins to leave their home?

"I just thought of something that might sweeten a move to town." Kelly's eyes sparkled as she looked at Abby. "Is there a quilting group locally?"

"Buffalo Gap has three quilting groups." Abby grinned. "We're a busy bunch. Some of the quilts come to Family Ties as gifts for the moms or the babies who are to be adopted. Some we donate to charities, and some are given to the local seniors, nursing homes, pediatric wards, etc. We're always looking for new members."

"Quilting is the love of my mom's life," Kelly said. "If she was in town, she'd be able to get involved, even join a group. But not without someone to watch Dad." Kelly blinked when Sam started laughing. "What's so funny?"

"The answer is Hilda Vermeer—no, her name is Cramer now because she married Joel Cramer," he explained then realized the explanation wouldn't help newcomer Kelly. "Hilda used to take in foster kids for Abby, but she hasn't had any lately. She told me after the funeral that she's bored and asked if there was some way she could help us out."

"Perfect. She'd be great with Kelly's father," Abby said.

"Hilda can talk to anyone about anything. Her arthritis bothers her hands, so she's dropped out of her quilt group, but I know she'd still like to feel useful." She wrinkled her nose. "I haven't placed any kids with her lately because of her hands and because I thought she and Joel should have time together after their recent marriage. But with Joel helping at his daughter-in-law's ranch, Hilda has lots of spare time. She lives in town, so it wouldn't be hard for her to come to your mom's on short notice."

"Hilda's not playing for the choir anymore?" Sam asked.

"Apparently, it's too much for her hands." Abby lifted an eyebrow. "What do you think, Kelly?"

"I think God has prepared a way for us to do this." Kelly smiled at Sam so warmly he felt a foot taller. "But someone other than me will have to suggest it. Mom will think I'm trying to boot her out of Marina's house."

"Arabella has a bug about Kelly," Sam explained to Abby. "We're not sure why, but it doesn't make life easier with the twins listening to everything."

"I'll ask Mayor Marsha to find out if the Emersons will consider selling. If so, I'll present the idea to Kelly's mom," Abby offered. "Or maybe I'll suggest she'd be doing them a favor by house-sitting and then let it slip that they want to move permanently."

"I'll make sure Mom knows about the quilting group first." Kelly grinned at Sam. "Might as well plant the desire before you offer a solution."

"Some people might say you're devious," he teased.

"Just using the brains God gave me." She winked at him. It took Abby clearing her throat for Sam to snap out of the spell that wink placed him in.

"Okay, that's our plan. I'll get working on my part right away. Thanks, Abby," he said and meant it. "Know that I'll do whatever I have to in order to ensure the twins stay where they belong."

"I will, too," Kelly agreed.

"As will I. The twins belong here where they've already established roots. It's clear that you both love them." Abby smiled. "Mind if I ask God to bless our plans?"

Sam bowed his head, though he wasn't sure her prayer would do any good. But just in case—he added one silent plea of his own. *Please?*

Once Abby had left, he and Kelly walked back to Marina and Jake's house. Arabella was sitting in the kitchen watching Jake's mom stir milk she was heating for cocoa.

"It's not the best thing for a child before bedtime," Arabella insisted.

"We always have it on Saturday night," Sadie told her. She caught sight of Sam and said, "It's our fam'ly t'dishon, right, Uncle Sam?"

"Your what?" Arabella frowned.

"Tradition. You're right, sweetie. Cocoa and a movie on Saturday night is a winter family tradition on the Triple D," he said more loudly than he intended, grateful they'd returned before Arabella could ruin the evening. "My mouth's watering already."

"Guess what, Mom?" Kelly stepped into the breach of Arabella's disapproving silence. "Abby was just telling me about some quilting groups in Buffalo Gap." She paused. "I had no idea they had such a demand for quilts here. It seems they're donated to a number of charitable causes. Sam says Abby is an amazing quilter and she has a long-arm machine."

"An *accomplished* quilting group?" Arabella asked.

"So I've heard," Kelly said with another wink at Sam as her mother lapsed into thought. This time it took Sadie yanking on his leg before Sam could break eye contact with Kelly.

Some strange connection flickered back and forth between them, something he didn't yet understand. He did know he was glad Kelly was staying. As he hunkered down to listen to Sadie, Sam realized that Kelly didn't seem like a guest at the ranch. It seemed to him that like the twins and Jacob Samuel, Kelly belonged with him on the Triple D.

Kelly blinked to clear her eyes as the credits rolled on the sappily sweet movie. She paused when she caught Sam watching her and knew from his lopsided grin that he'd seen her weeping.

"Softie," he murmured with a gently mocking grin.

"That movie made even you teary eyed a couple of times," she insisted. "You can't deny it."

"Of course I can. I'm a rancher," he snorted. "We don't get teary eyed." His scoff of disgust roused Jacob Samuel from his comfy position on Sam's chest. Immediately, the big rancher's face softened, and he used a soothing pat on the baby's back.

"Big and tough, all right," Kelly teased softly, enjoying the sight of this tough muscular man lovingly caring for a baby.

"Well, what about you, dedicated career woman?" Sam shot back. "You look right at home sitting there with the girls. Your hair's all mussed and there's popcorn butter on your cheek." He chuckled when she eased her hand out from behind Emma to brush her cheek.

"We're saps for these guys, aren't we?" Kelly brushed Sadie's bangs off her face and pressed a kiss against her brow then smiled at Sam. "Besotted, that's what we are."

"Yep." His voice sounded lower, more gravelly. He didn't look directly at her before rising, careful not to jar the baby. "I'm going to tuck this little guy in his crib, then I'll come and help you with those two."

"Thanks." She smiled dreamily at Sam, comparing him to the hero in the movie who risked life and limb to save a young boy from people determined to harm him.

"Do I have butter on my face, too?" he asked, one eyebrow arched in a query.

"No." Kelly felt the heat burn her cheeks and quickly averted her gaze to the handmade quilt he'd spread over them earlier.

"Then what?" he asked.

Sam was good-looking enough to star in any movie, but she had no intention of saying that aloud. Feeling awkward, as if a sudden intimacy had grown between them, she was almost relieved when her mother wandered into the room.

"Are those children still up?" she demanded.

"No, Mom. As you can see, they're sleeping. We're about to put them to bed." Kelly noted Sam leaving the room while she was still speaking. A moment later he returned, his arms empty.

"Did you need something, Arabella?" he asked pleasantly as he lifted away the quilt that covered Kelly and the twins and folded it.

"I made that for Marina." Arabella's voice wobbled. "She was so good at taking pictures and drawing and handcrafts, but she never really took to quilting."

"I'm sure she appreciated it." Kelly could only pray this wouldn't turn into another diatribe. "The backing is so cozy."

"It's a special kind of chenille," her mother said in a pleasant conversational tone. Then she caught herself. "But why am I telling you? You don't quilt, either." She sighed then turned toward the kitchen. "Your father wants a drink of water. He seems very unsettled tonight."

"I'm sorry." This was her own mother, and Kelly didn't know what to say to her. She was afraid to say anything, lest she trigger unpleasantness. So she remained silent.

"It's probably because of that cocoa everyone insisted he drink." Arabella tossed a glare at Sam.

Thankfully, he simply offered a quiet, "I'm sorry."

When her mother passed through with a glass of water, Kelly said good-night, but the only response was a passing glare Arabella tossed at the still-sleeping girls before stomping her way upstairs. The thud of the bedroom door wasn't enough to wake Jacob Samuel but it was distinctly audible.

"I wish I could figure out what's upsetting her so. She's never been a particularly happy person, but this—" Kelly shook her head then frowned at Sam. "Was she as bad before I came?"

The answer was clear from the dour look he gave her, but all Sam said was, "She's had a rough time. First your dad's diagnosis, then losing Marina, selling her home. She just needs space and some time to settle in to her new life. Now we'd better get these two to bed so they can get up for church tomorrow morning."

"You're going to church?" Kelly wasn't sure why, but she'd somehow assumed it was the last place he'd go, that he'd made an exception because of the funeral but—

"Jake and Marina made sure the kids went to Sunday school every week. They all sat together for the morning service." His green eyes grew dark and shadowed. "My brother was adamant about raising his kids in the faith he cherished. I have to honor that."

"Even though you don't believe the same?" Kelly waited curiously for his response.

"Oh, I believe in God." Sam crossed his arms over his chest, his chin thrusting out as he spoke. "I believe He's in control and He can do whatever He wants. Where it falls apart for me is that He doesn't use His power to stop horrible things from happening. And He could."

Then, as if Sam didn't want to discuss it anymore, he leaned forward and brushed his hand against Sadie's cheek. Kelly sat listening and watching as he tenderly roused the little girl just enough to coax her into his arms then carried her to her room. Kelly could have done the same for Emma. Instead, she stayed where she was and waited for Sam's return, profoundly moved by his heartfelt affection for the twins. His actions only affirmed what she'd decided the first day she'd arrived at the Triple D.

The children belonged with Sam. He loved them so much, was even willing to set aside his beliefs to ensure they had the spiritual upbringing their parents wanted. He was a born father. He should have these children for his own, no question.

"I'm glad you insisted they put on their pajamas before the movie," he said when he returned the second time. "They fell back to sleep right away."

"Good." Kelly rose and began gathering the cocoa and popcorn dishes until Sam's hand closed over hers, stopping her. Stomach shivering from the contact, she drew back as she looked at him questioningly.

"Go to bed, Kelly. Morning comes early for you," he said in the same fond voice he'd used with the girls. He gently freed the dishes from her grip.

"You should talk. You were up awfully early yourself." She trailed behind him into the kitchen. "You're running the ranch as well as doing a lot of stuff here, too. I wish you'd tell me what else I could do to help. I'm here to carry part of the load with you, Sam, but I can't unless you tell me what else I should be doing."

"What else?" Having dried his hands on the dish towel, he tossed it to the counter and turned to face her, grinning as he shook his head. "Kelly, you've already taken on far more than I ever intended, including all the cooking, and I want you to know I appreciate it."

"Looking after three kids, one of whom naps twice a day, isn't that hard." How could anyone resist Sam's smile?

"I know exactly how hard it is, Kelly," he said. "Your sister often shared how tired she was when the twins' mischief wore her down, never mind the added chores of cleaning and feeding extra people. I know it's not easy, but if it makes you feel better," he said, amusement threading his words, "I'll let you know when I need more help with the ranch."

When, she noted. Not *if*. Meaning he was expecting some turbulent times ahead?

"You do that." Kelly held his gaze to show him she was serious. "I may only be here for six months and I'm clueless at ranching, but I could hold a calf or something if you need it."

"Thank you," he said, lips twitching.

"I mean it," Kelly insisted. "I only make plain food, and I'm sure I'm nowhere near as good at mothering as Marina was, but I want to do everything I can to keep this place a home where the kids still feel loved and safe."

"You're already doing that." Sam's voice turned low, introspective. "Marina would be proud of you."

"As Jake would be of you," she returned, glimpsing a flicker of doubt cross his face. "It's true. I'm sure he knew he couldn't have chosen a better dad for his kids."

Sam's smile stretched even wider. Kelly caught her breath and then stopped breathing altogether when his hand cupped her cheek.

"You're a very sweet woman, Kelly Krause. Thank you. For everything." He leaned forward and brushed his lips against her cheek in a gentle kiss. "Now go to bed. I'll turn out the lights and lock up as I leave. Good night."

"Good night, Sam." Dazed by his touch, Kelly glided upstairs to check on the twins, praying that her parents were asleep and her mother wouldn't hear the creak of the top stair and come to investigate.

But once Kelly was lying in her own bed, she couldn't sleep. After half an hour of tossing, she finally rose, checked on the kids again then bundled up in an old bathrobe of Marina's and sat on her window seat, where she could look out over the Triple D.

The moon rose full and bright, casting a brilliant glow across the snow, illuminating the dark stands of evergreens, cattle scattered over the sloping hills and the tiny valley where hopefully a stream would soon melt and flow. She tried to fix the image in her mind so that when she got a free moment, she could start transferring it to one of the fabric pictures she loved to create.

A flicker of motion in front of the log house across the yard nudged her back to awareness. Sam emerged clad in his thick sheepskin coat. He wore his brown Stetson tilted at the familiar jaunty angle as he strode to the barn, where she knew some of the newest calves had been moved inside after Sam had found recent signs of a wolf pack prowling nearby.

Sam opened the barn door and disappeared inside. Kelly didn't know how much time elapsed. She was too busy remembering his face when he'd talked about God not doing anything to stop bad things from happening.

"Sam loves you," she whispered to the heavenly Father on whom she'd learned to depend. "He's just hurt and confused and worried about losing the kids. Please help me help him protect and care for them. Please be there for him. And please—" This part was so hard to say. "Keep me immune to him. But if it's Your will, please let him keep the twins as Jake and Marina wanted."

Keeping in God's will—that was her goal. Sleep beckoned. Kelly smothered a yawn and was about to rise when Sam emerged from the barn and trudged back to the little log house she'd learned he built himself and now housed him and his parents. He paused on the doorstep, turned and surveyed Jake and Marina's house, where she was staying, his eyes resting on it, as if to reassure himself that the kids were still peacefully sleeping, that there was nothing more he could do for them tonight. Kelly wished she could see his face, discern what he was thinking. But then he opened his front door and disappeared inside. Dear Sam, making sure everything was right in the world.

Grateful for his strength and protection, Kelly climbed into her bed. But before she closed her eyes to sleep, she offered one last prayer.

"Please, Lord, please keep us just friends. I know Your will for me doesn't include a husband and family. I've learned that the hard way. So let me be content doing what I can to help Sam and the kids and help me be strong when it's time to go."

By contradiction, Kelly's dreams that night included her and Sam and the kids, laughing and playing in the snow. But when her eyes met his, it didn't seem to Kelly that they were just friends, not in her dream anyway.

Chapter Five

Kelly enjoyed attending Sunday service with Sam and the kids. She wasn't used to being among people who knew so much about her personally, but there was no way to worship incognito in the Buffalo Gap congregation when everyone greeted her by name. Funny thing was, Kelly liked the sense of camaraderie their friendliness offered. She enjoyed the lesson on giving, but not as much as she liked the way Sam's shoulder rubbed against hers as they sat beside each other in the fireside room.

Maybe liked it too much?

When Sunday school concluded, Sam left to bring the twins from their classroom back to the sanctuary. Having wondered how they'd fare without their parents, Kelly heaved a sigh of relief at the happy smiles wreathing their faces as they took their place on the pew beside her. Sam sat next to Kelly then lifted Jacob Samuel from her arms, his shoulder rubbing hers as he settled the child on his knee. On the other side of the twins, Sam's parents took their place. Kelly scanned the room and saw her parents seated at the back of the sanctuary.

She knew from the commiserating looks sent their way that this was Jake and Marina's family pew, and for a few moments sadness threatened to overwhelm her until she realized that Jake and Marina were worshipping with God, in His very presence.

This service felt different than the ones Kelly usually attended on the ship. For one thing, during the prelude people stopped by, smiled at her, spoke with Sam or his parents and offered fond words for the kids.

Sam didn't have to say or do anything for Kelly to know he'd have preferred to be anywhere but in this church, just as no one had to explain to her that his reasons had to do with his past and the fiancée he still mourned. Kelly knew Naomi must have been a very special woman, because Sam clearly still loved her. Perhaps that was why her loss affected him so deeply.

The song leader opened the service with a lively chorus. As the congregation rose and joined in the hymn singing, as they bowed their heads for prayer then listened to the visiting missionary's stories, Kelly felt a strong reassurance that God was here, waiting to lead her through this uncharted territory as He had so many times before. By the time the meeting concluded, she felt comforted and able to leave refreshed.

"You're Kelly, right?" A woman about her own age with short coppery hair and green eyes that danced with fun stopped her in the foyer. She thrust out a hand and grinned. "I'm Sheena Parks."

"It's nice to meet you," Kelly said as she shook the diminutive woman's hand.

"It's nicer to meet you." Sheena chuckled at Kelly's surprised look. "Marina once told me that you're a port consultant with a cruise line."

Kelly nodded.

"So you've traveled a lot." Sheena waited for her nod. "I was wondering if you might be willing to come and talk to me about it. Oh, I should have said I run the local travel agency. I've got some clients who want to visit destinations

I don't know very well. I usually like to offer tips and suggestions to my customers, but I don't have any for these places. I hoped you might have some suggestions for me."

"Sure, though I don't know if I'll be much help," Kelly said, noting that Sam was busy helping the twins into their coats. "Where do they want to go?"

"Greece and Australia." Sheena arched one coppery eyebrow. "You've been to both, right?"

"Many times." Kelly liked this woman. It could be fun to share stories about her travels, but she sensed Sam was impatient to get away so she asked for Sheena's phone number. "I'm mostly tied up with the kids but maybe I could give you a call if I have some free time."

"Great. You could bring the kids to my office," Sheena said with a glance at Sam and the waiting children. "I have a raft of toys in an area where they can play to their hearts' content." She handed Kelly a business card. "Call anytime. I'd love to get together. See you." She lifted a hand then hurried away to speak to someone else.

"Take a deep breath," Sam advised in an amused voice from behind her. Kelly turned, found him nearer than she'd expected. "Talking to Sheena's a bit like contact with a tornado. Are you ready to leave?"

"Just have to get my coat. Oh," she said as Sam held it, waiting for her to slide her arms inside. "Thank you. I'll get Jacob Samuel from your mom and then we can go."

She made a game of racing the twins to the truck, which thankfully was running and toasty warm inside. On the ride home, Sadie informed Emma that they'd need Sam's help to build their planned snow fort.

"It's too cold to play outside this afternoon," Sam interjected. "You'll have to think up some indoor games." Silence followed his words, then a rush of whispering began that lasted until they pulled up in front of the ranch house.

Across the yard at Sam's house, Kelly noticed that his parents' car hadn't returned.

"They always go out for Sunday brunch with friends," he told her. "They won't be back for a while."

"We'll build a fort with Grannybell's quilt," Sadie told him as she snapped off her seat belt and raced inside.

"I'm still waiting for that famous Alberta chinook, Sam." Kelly shivered as she hurried to the door of Marina's house, glad for Sam's helping hand under her arm as they crossed the slippery parts of the path. With his other hand Sam snuggled Jacob Samuel's head into his chest to protect his delicate face from the bitter wind.

"Waiting is what we do here. Don't you know this is next year country?" Sam chuckled at her moue of disgust and recited, "Next year the herds will be bigger. Next year the crops will be better. Next year we'll have more money in the bank. That's the rancher's song. Anybody who's got half a brain would give up ranching for the oil patch."

"Really?' She paused at the door and waved a hand to encompass the snow-covered rolling hills around them. "You'd rather look at oil wells than this?"

"Nah." He stepped past her with a grin. Inside the porch he moved his hand so Jacob Samuel could see. "But I'd sure like to have the paychecks."

"The ranch isn't doing well?" Kelly hadn't given finances a thought, but now she wondered…

"Lose that scared look, Kelly," Sam ordered. "The Triple D is fine, but I've never met a rancher yet who didn't want more money in the bank to fall back on in lean times." He sniffed. "Something smells amazing. I'm starved."

"Nothing new there," she said, tongue in cheek. Once she'd shed her own outerwear, she began to free Jacob Samuel from his snowsuit. "It's chili in the slow cooker. Want to make a salad?"

"Me?" Sam's hands froze on the zipper of his jacket.

Something that looked a lot like fear crept across his face. He tugged the zipper back up. "Maybe I should—"

"Your cows are fine," Kelly said firmly, suppressing her amusement. "Take off your jacket and I'll give you directions while I ice the cake I made this morning."

"Cake?" Sam needed only a second to think that over. "Okay." He took off his jacket and rubbed his hands. "But maybe I should ice the cake."

"You know how to make icing?" Kelly asked, keeping her face blank.

"Salad it is. Which I'm guessing means lettuce?" He set the baby in his high chair then opened the fridge door and peered inside for what seemed like ages to Kelly.

She reached past him, removed the head of lettuce from the crisper and set it on the counter. "Green onions, celery, tomatoes, too. In the other drawer," she said. "On the bottom."

Irritated when he didn't immediately select the items but determined not to rescue him, she pulled out the mixer and assembled her ingredients for icing. He finally closed the fridge door.

"Now what?" Sam asked.

"I prewashed all the ingredients. You could start by cutting up the celery," she suggested then added, "In small pieces," when he pulled out the biggest knife in the block.

It seemed to Kelly that it took forever for Sam to make his salad. She finished icing her cake, set the table, boiled the kettle for tea and added a few more spices to her chili. There was even time to chat with her mom as she shed her coat before he pronounced his creation finished. Kelly offered praise for his work, though there was enough salad for twenty people.

Once everyone was seated at the table, Kelly's father insisted they hold hands while he said grace. Kelly slid her hand into Sam's, quashing the burst of sensation that tickled up her arm and reminding herself she was too old for crushes. That didn't stop her from stealing several glances at him all through the meal.

"Delicious." Sam savored his third helping of chili with gusto. "It sure goes well with my salad, which, by the way, is also amazing."

"It certainly is large enough for another meal or two," Arabella said then frowned. "I didn't know you could cook, Kelly. You never did much at home."

"Didn't want to compete with a pro, Mom," Kelly said and smiled. "Your meals were always gourmet. I hesitated to offer my feeble efforts."

"I wish you would have," Arabella said. "I'd have gladly relinquished my position. I never enjoyed cooking."

"But you spent hours perfecting recipes." Kelly stared at her, shocked by her confession.

"Because that's what my friends did." Arabella sipped her tea. "I much preferred to work on my quilts, but that wasn't popular back then."

So she'd made herself spend hours in the kitchen? Kelly needed time to process that information.

"It's quite good chili," Arabella complimented. "Not like Marina's. She threw in anything at hand. She didn't care for cooking, either."

"She made some delicious meals," Sam defended.

"Yes." Arabella nodded, her face thoughtful. "But my daughter was always far happier with her baby boy and her cameras than she was in the kitchen." Her smile faded and she stared at her plate.

"I always liked your peach pie." Neil's quiet voice broke the silence that had fallen. He covered his wife's hand with his own. "Nobody can make a peach pie like you, Arabella."

Kelly gulped at the rush of love that flowed from her mother to her father when she smiled and patted his hand, and wondered how long it would be before her father couldn't remember their shared past. Would she still be here?

"Thank you, dear. I'm glad you enjoyed it. Perhaps I'll make you a fresh peach pie this summer," Arabella said in a tender voice Kelly hadn't heard in many years.

Suddenly, she felt someone watching her. She lifted her head and caught Sam studying her. When he smiled, something passed between them, some invisible thread that held her spellbound and wouldn't let her look away.

"Are we havin' that cake for d'sert?" Sadie's inquisitive gaze moved from Sam to Kelly. "You two look funny," she said. "Did that salad make your tummy no good?"

The comment, added to the scrutiny of the others at the table suddenly turned on them, made Kelly blush. She gulped, forced a laugh then said, "My tummy is good, thanks, Sadie. And yes, that cake is certainly for dessert. Have you had enough chili?"

"Uh-huh. It was good." The little girl climbed out of her booster seat and carried her plate to the counter. Then she took Emma's and Sam's plates and lastly her grandparents'. That task completed, she returned to her seat and grinned at Kelly. "We're all ready for the d'sert."

"Thank you, sweetie. That's very helpful." Kelly shot a dark look at Sam, whose shoulders shook with suppressed laughter. She carried her own plate to the counter and returned with the cake and a stack of dishes.

"It looks too pretty to cut," Emma whispered.

"Thank you, Emma. That's such a nice compliment." Kelly smiled at her and held out the table knife. "Would you like to cut it?"

Emma's eyes stretched wide. "Can I?" she asked in a breathless voice.

"I want to." Sadie jumped to her feet and hurried around the table to stand at Kelly's elbow. "I'll do it," she insisted.

Kelly wasn't sure what to do as Emma's face fell. Thankfully, she didn't have to do anything because Sam intervened.

"Kelly asked Emma," he said quietly. "Maybe you can cut it next time, Sadie."

"No. Emma can't." Sadie glared at him, her blue eyes angry, her posture tense. "I want to do it."

"Sit down at the table, Sadie. Emma will cut the cake." Sam's voice brooked no argument, though it was neither raised nor louder. It was, however, very clear that he was serious.

Sadie stood her ground for several moments, glaring at him. When she finally accepted that Sam wouldn't change his mind, she stomped back to her seat, pinching Emma on the way. Sam moved with lightning-quick reflexes, scooping Sadie from her chair and carrying her from the room amid loud protests. After their departure, silence reigned for a moment until Kelly beckoned to Emma.

"Come, Emma. It's time to taste whether this cake is any good." She watched the little girl hesitate, cast a glance toward the bedroom she shared with Sadie then shake her head.

"Sadie can cut it," she whispered.

"Sadie is all finished with lunch," Sam said in a calm voice as he returned to the table. "She's staying in her room for now."

That didn't seem to persuade Emma. She remained in her chair, refusing to move until Neil whispered, "Cut me a big piece, please, Emma? I love cake."

A tiny smile crept across her face as her eyes met his. Slowly, she slid out of her chair and walked around the table to Neil. "With lots of icing?" she said in her hushed voice.

"With lots of everything," he whispered back.

"Okay." Emma proceeded to cut the cake. But Kelly barely noticed as her gaze slid to Sam's.

Did you hear that? she asked without speaking aloud. *Emma spoke in a normal tone of voice. One word, but still.*

Sam nodded at her as if he understood exactly what she

meant. His sober glance rested on the little girl, watching as she cut cake then served some to everyone.

"This is for me?" he asked when Emma set a plate before him. She nodded. "Thank you. Is that piece for you?"

"Uh-uh. That's Sadie's," Emma murmured, back to her soft tone. "I don't want any."

"Oh, honey." Sam's sad look made the little girl frown. "Kelly made this cake for us. She's going to think you don't like it."

"I like cake, but—" Emma stared at the cake platter longingly. "Not t'day," she said stoutly.

"I wish you did." Sam sighed in a long-suffering manner. "I like sharing. I was hoping you and I could eat our cake together. Please?" he wheedled.

"Okay." Emma grinned and hopped up on his knee. "I gived you the biggest piece," she confided. "'Cause you're the bestest uncle in the whole world." Then she threw her arms around his neck and hugged him.

Thanks to Sam's adept handling of the situation, everyone, including Emma, was able to enjoy their dessert. Except Kelly. She couldn't stop thinking about the little girl in her bedroom who didn't have any cake. She ate only a tiny corner of her dessert, intending to save it for Sadie, but Sam caught on and when Emma left to talk to Neil, he moved the plate back in front of her.

"Sadie has to learn not to bully, Kelly," he murmured for her ears alone. "I'm even more convinced now that's what is at the root of Emma's whispering. It has to stop."

"I know." She took a small forkful of the cake. It tasted like dust.

"You're a softie, that's all." His grin didn't mock or tease. Instead, it seemed to Kelly that they shared a sweet moment of common thinking before he rose, obviously intending to leave the room.

"Not that soft," she said. "You're on cleanup duty. No

argument now. It sets a bad example." His mother and father had just stepped through the door and she burst out
laughing at Sam's chagrined look as he glanced at Emma
then began rinsing the plates Emma had cleared.

"I've been trying to get my son to help out in the kitchen
for nearly thirty years," Verna explained, eyes gaping as
she watched Sam work. "I don't know how you managed it,
Kelly, but I'm indebted. I've always believed children should
be raised knowing how to care for themselves."

"I care for myself," Sam protested with a pseudohurt look.

"TV dinners and eating out the rest of the time are not
caring for yourself. You work hard, son. You need to eat
nutritiously. I won't always be there to cook for you." She
winked at Kelly. "No wife wants a man who can't handle
a little kitchen duty."

"I don't have a wife, Mother," Sam pointed out.

"Exactly my point." Verna nudged Jock. "You can help
him. Neil, too. The females are taking a break from KP."
She took Arabella's hand on one side and Kelly's on the
other and scooted Emma in front of them out of the kitchen.

"Kelly, where's your 'feel sorry' for me?" Sam asked
before she left.

"At the bottom of that bowl of salad, I think," she mumbled. She glanced over her shoulder. "I don't want to be a
softie," she shot back with a smug smile. "Besides," she
added very quietly, "you said you like sharing."

His groan followed her into the living room.

Wasn't it fun to laugh and share with Sam?

This, Kelly decided, was what home should feel like.

Sam brought Sadie from her room once he'd finished
cleaning the kitchen, but not before he explained about how
she'd made Emma feel. Sadie asked him a hundred questions of course, but in the end Sam was confident she understood that a repeat of her behavior would be punished.

But the twins were bored. Kelly had put Jacob Samuel down for his nap and had to return to resettle him twice when the girls' rowdiness disturbed him.

"I'm running out of ideas to entertain them," he confided to Kelly when Arabella and Neil had retired to escape the mayhem, though they said it was to rest. His parents had gone to his place claiming the same thing. "Any suggestions?"

Kelly's lovely brown eyes met his. She nodded slowly. "I might have. But I need twenty minutes or so to prepare."

"I can do twenty minutes more. I think." He managed, but by the end of it, Sam was bone tired and a little frustrated that all his former tactics weren't keeping the girls entertained. Thankfully, Kelly returned, her arms laden with materials.

"What's all this?" he asked, taking some of the things from her and setting them on the table.

"Well, I thought maybe the twins could help me make an album of these pictures I have."

Though Sam knew Kelly was speaking to the twins, the display of photos she was arranging tweaked his interest big-time.

"You want to make a picture book like the mish-nary had at church today?" Sadie asked.

"Yes. Sort of." Kelly smiled at the little girl then tapped the tip of her nose with one finger. "Would you and Emma mind helping me?"

"We don't mind," Sadie assured her after a quick look at Emma, who nodded then asked, "An' Uncle Sam, too?"

"Of course Uncle Sam can help us, if he wants to." Kelly looked straight at him, a question in her dark brown eyes.

Sometimes he felt she was intentionally putting a distance between them. He attributed it to her determination to find her own way to deal with the twins. Or maybe he was making something out of nothing. Lately, he'd been coming and going so much now that calving was in full swing. Sam got preoccupied with constantly checking on the mums and the new arrivals.

At least Sam hoped he was wrong and everything was okay with Kelly. She'd had to make a big adjustment to the twins' constant questions and Jacob Samuel's loud demands, but he thought she was managing. He hoped.

"Where are the pictures from?" He leaned next to her to study them more closely.

"Australia and New Zealand. I hope you don't mind. I borrowed Marina's equipment to print them. She has a fantastic setup for photos. Had," she corrected softly. A mistiness passed through her eyes, but she blinked it away.

"That is a kangaroo," he told Emma, who seemed entranced by the picture.

"Wallaby," Kelly corrected. "A common mistake. Wallabies are a little smaller than kangaroos and more colorful."

"Okay, but I know that's a koala." Sam couldn't seem to tear his gaze from the photo of the baby animal with its arms around Kelly's neck. "I always planned to go and see them." The words slipped out of his mouth without thinking.

"I loved them," Kelly murmured, a certain wistfulness on her face.

"You look very happy. It must have been a wonderful day." He wondered if there was another reason she was grinning so widely for the camera. "Who took the picture?"

"Just—a friend." Her slight hesitation before the last two words told him that friend had meant a lot to her.

"Do you still keep in touch?" Sam asked then chided himself for prying. It was none of his business, and yet he couldn't suppress his curiosity.

"Not really." She moved away from him, but the soft floral scent of her perfume lingered like the hint of sadness that clung to her voice. "We served a term on board together, but he's married now, with a family. He lives in Turkey." She caught her breath then explained to the girls, "This picture was taken in a faraway place called Australia." She glanced at Sam then at the photos. "I was there often but not for a long time. But it was really fun."

"Mostly because it was warm?" he teased, chuckling when he saw the truth flush her face. "How many sweaters are you wearing today?"

"Three," she admitted. "I can't seem to warm up."

"No wonder. It's cool in here." Sam rose, walked to the thermostat and frowned. "It's not even at 70."

"I didn't want to run up your energy bill. Mom said heating is pricey out here," Kelly said.

Sam couldn't hide the grimace that twisted his lips. Arabella said too much. Couldn't God do something, help her move?

"I was trying to save you a few dollars," she defended.

"Kelly, we're not broke. We can afford to heat the house," he said, his voice unintentionally stern. His gaze held hers for a long moment before he turned away and flicked the dial upward. Immediately, the furnace kicked in. "Don't take Arabella's word. I'll tell you if we need to cut back, and the first thing won't be heat."

She nodded. Sam watched the warmth filling the room chase away her chills. He swallowed his irritation, wondering what else she was cutting back on because of Arabella.

"Tell me if you need something." He'd better check the grocery stocks. Kelly preferred her coffee stronger than the brew her mother made, and she always added a splash of cream. She also favored fresh fruit and vegetables to frozen or canned. They weren't cheap in winter, but Sam's mother had told him Kelly was determined to make the kids' diets nutrient rich.

"How do we start making the book?" Sadie asked.

Sam observed as Kelly organized supplies she must have

found in Marina's office. He made sure a car was available whenever she needed it, but Kelly had only been to town once. She must have bought the two photo albums then.

"I thought you girls could glue the pictures in the books. There are two of everything so you can each make your own book," she explained. "You can clip and arrange them any way you like. Uncle Sam and I will help if you need it."

Hoping this exercise would fill in some time, Sam left to make coffee. When he returned with two steaming mugs, he could see the twins were enjoying using their glue sticks and plastic scissors to fill their books.

"Here's a cup of coffee. I hope I put in enough cream." He watched her taste it.

"Perfect," Kelly said with a smile. "I needed this." She listened to Emma's quiet question about a particular photo. "That's Ayers Rock. It's a huge piece of stone that sticks out of the ground. Lots of people go to see it and climb up it."

"I want to go there," Sadie said, thumping on her picture to make it stick.

"Me, too," Sam agreed almost under his breath.

"Perhaps one day you will." Kelly's quiet tone seemed directed at Sadie, but her glance rested on him. "If you do, don't miss the sunrise," she murmured. "It's spectacular. One of the area's Aboriginal people showed me a fantastic spot to see it."

"You should do a presentation at the high school one day," he said. "Or maybe at the seniors' hall. People in Buffalo Gap are starting to travel more widely."

"Sheena asked if she could call me with questions her clients have," Kelly confided. "I agreed, though I'm not sure she needs my help. She seems very knowledgeable."

"Sheena traveled a fair bit with her sister, but that was several years ago," Sam said in a quiet voice. "I thought she'd lost interest in traveling by herself."

He and Naomi had talked long and often about traveling. Guilt suffused him as he realized he could no longer visualize Naomi's face without looking at her picture. The thought shamed Sam. He'd loved her; why couldn't he remember her?

"I hope she starts again," Kelly said. "Travel certainly broadens your horizons."

"I doubt Sheena ever went to as many places as you," Sam said with a grin. "But she shares your yen for warmer climes."

"What's a clime?" Sadie wanted to know.

"A warmer clime is where your auntie Kel goes, so she doesn't have to wear three sweaters to keep warm. Oh, two sweaters. She's taken one off." Sam chuckled when Kelly glowered at him. "Are you two going to finish putting all these pictures in your books today?"

"Yes." Emma at least had no doubt.

Sam leaned back in his chair and sipped his coffee, finding a sweet contentment in the sight of the two girls squabbling amicably over whose book would look the best. He pushed away the wayward reflection that it was Kelly's presence that kept him there.

By the time Jacob Samuel woke from his afternoon nap, the albums were finished and the twins had moved on to creating their own Ayers Rock with blocks. Kelly removed the bits of glue the twins hadn't cleaned off the table while Sam changed the baby, got him a bottle then returned to sit at the table with him, watching Kelly assemble scraps of fabric from a bag.

"What are you doing?" he asked curiously after she'd rejected more bits of cloth than she'd accepted.

"Choosing what I'll use in my next quilt," Kelly explained.

"You quilt, too?" Sam shook his head. "The ladies around here are going to love you. Ever since Abby came to town and got a quilt group started, the females of Buffalo Gap have gone nuts about quilting."

"So I've heard. But they make much larger quilts than me. I do pictures. They're called art quilts, but they're small so they're not really quilts at all. I like them because I can do them on the ship. All I need is a simple sewing machine, some colored thread and some fabric bits. Marina has, had—" She stopped, swallowed.

Sam could see from the wince she gave that it still hurt to say her sister's name. "Go on," he encouraged.

"I brought some stuff along to start a new project. Marina's pictures gave me an idea," Kelly explained. "I thought I'd do a picture of the kids."

Sam questioned her extensively about the process, intrigued by her craft.

"I'll be interested in seeing the end product." He glanced around. "By the way, thank you for putting Marina's pictures back up. It didn't feel like a home without them."

"The girls told me that I didn't put them up exactly as they were." Kelly shrugged. "I did my best. I'm glad you don't mind what I've done."

"Mind? I'm very glad you did," Sam told her as a little glow of warmth flamed at having this house returned to a home, though he knew perfectly well that didn't only have to do with the pictures. A lot of that feeling of warmth came from Kelly's presence here.

"I think it's important for them to have familiar things in place." Kelly smiled at him.

"Exactly." As her smile added to that cozy feeling inside, Sam chided himself to step back. Kelly was a friend, a good one. But that was all. Losing Naomi had made him determined never to suffer that intense pain of loss again.

Not that Kelly seemed to want a relationship. He wondered why.

"I'm hungry." Sadie leaned against Sam's knee. "What's for supper, Uncle Sam?"

"Ask Auntie Kel. She cooks way better than I do." He

grinned when Kelly lifted one eyebrow at him. "I'll do cleanup."

"Promises, promises." Kelly made a grumpy face. "Like you promised the same last night then left to check on a cow? Or this morning when another cow emergency called you away and I had to clean up all that bacon grease?" She shook her head. "I only look gullible, Sam. You're on supper detail."

"She's a tough one, Sadie Lady." Sam handed the baby to Kelly then reached out for the little girl's hand. "You and I better go check out the fridge and see what we can burn for supper."

"But I don't like burned supper," Sadie mourned. She turned to Kelly. "Please will you help Uncle Sam make us supper? Burned food tastes bad."

"Very bad," Emma agreed in an almost whisper.

"Yeah," Sam added with the most plaintive sigh. "Awful."

"Oh, come on, Sam. You must cook for yourself," Kelly sputtered, obviously indignant that he'd use the kids to con her.

"Canned soup, pork and beans, eat out." Sam ticked them off on his fingers.

"I hate soup," Sadie said, planting her feet firmly apart and glaring at Kelly.

"I don't like beans," Emma murmured, then her blue eyes brightened. "Can we go to Gran's?"

"No. Gran's not feeling well. Flu, I think." Sam sighed then shrugged at Kelly. "Maybe she has something in the freezer."

"Don't bother your mother," she said in exasperation. "I put out some ground turkey to thaw for tacos. You can cook it, Sadie can grate the cheese and Emma can cut up the tomatoes."

"I don't want to grate cheese," Sadie whined. "It hurts my fingers."

"T'matoes make me 'llergic," Emma added.

"Okay, so Emma does the cheese and Sadie cuts tomatoes." Kelly sounded frustrated. "If you want to eat, you have to work together."

Sam gazed at her helplessly. Even Jacob Samuel started to blubber. A rush of hope rose. Maybe if he went about this the right way, Kelly would give in to the urge he could read so clearly on her face to shoo them all away and prepare the meal herself. It would be quicker and cleaner, and he wouldn't have to embarrass himself by displaying his ineptitude in the kitchen. He dropped that idea when Kelly shook her head.

"It won't work, Sam," she said sternly. "I can't go to town for the afternoon or anywhere else," she said with emphasis on the *anywhere*, "knowing that if I was late, you couldn't feed the kids, so roll up your sleeves."

Sam sighed and rose. He leaned toward Kelly when she beckoned him closer with one fingertip.

"What kind of an impression will it make on a social worker if their caregiver can't even feed his family properly?" she said in a voice too low for the twins to hear. "I'm here to help this family gain independence."

"Where do I start?" he asked, admitting defeat.

"At the beginning. Come on, girls. You, too, little one." Kelly grinned at Jacob Samuel, who was now gnawing on his fist, and laughed. "I can see you're starving, so while I feed you, the others will have a cooking lesson."

Sam forced himself to stop gawking at the beautiful woman in front of him and concentrate on supper. It wasn't easy. For the next hour Kelly alternated between laughing exasperation and smug satisfaction as he learned how to chop and sauté onions before adding the meat and spices. Though the twins grumbled at first, Sam's proud success encouraged them to pitch in to do their part of making the meal.

Finally, everything was on the table. The lettuce wasn't

exactly shredded, the cheese resembled large marbles and the tomatoes—well, frankly, the tomatoes were almost mush. But nobody complained, except Arabella. The twins barely lasted through a short grace before they began stuffing ingredients into hard taco shells and trying to wrap their lips around it. Sam didn't think he'd ever tasted anything so good.

"The twins and I made dinner," he told Kelly's parents proudly.

"I can see someone's been busy." Arabella gave a dour look at the messy counters. "Cleanup should be fun."

"What can we make t'morrow?" Sadie's face bore smears of taco sauce, and her plate was nearly empty.

Emma murmured something. Sam blinked with surprise. Emma seldom volunteered anything.

"What was that, Emma?" Kelly shook her head when Sadie seemed about to answer. "I want Emma to tell me." She smiled at the little girl to encourage her to speak. They all waited.

Sam was about to give up on her when she whispered, "Pasgetti."

"Spaghetti?" Emma nodded. "You like pasta?"

"I like pasgetti," Emma repeated in the faintest whisper.

"Me, too," Sam added with a grin. "With garlic bread."

"An' meatballs," Sadie added, her smile wide.

"Since we had hamburger in our chili lunch, I suggest we should wait a day or two before we have it again," Kelly said.

"You're telling a rancher not to eat beef?" Sam grinned. "Them's fightin' words, lady."

"I didn't mean—" She blushed beautifully when he chuckled. "Stop teasing me," she ordered, but her smile spoiled her severe tone.

Sam liked that smile. He liked it a lot.

Chapter Six

Why was it that Sam could make her heart race with just a smile?

"Variety is the spice of life." Kelly glanced around the supper table, struggling to regain her composure. "How about if we plan a menu for each day so we make sure to cook everyone's favorites? We could do it tonight after we have dessert."

"D'sert?" The girls looked at each other, eyes wide. "We're having d'sert?" Sadie's searching gaze scanned the kitchen counters. "What?"

"Pie?" Sam's hopeful green gaze made Kelly's stomach tighten.

"Did you guys make pie?" Kelly teased. The sad way they shook their heads, Sam's the saddest shake of all, made her giggle. "We'll have to plan dessert in our menu, also. For tonight, why don't we have some canned peaches?"

"That's Mommy's go-to d'sert." Suddenly, Sadie was in tears. "I miss my mommy," she wailed. Emma sobbed silently beside her.

Kelly's heart swelled with pride as Sam immediately rose and moved between the girls' chairs. He looped his arms around each shoulder and hugged them close.

"It's okay," he soothed. "Mommy and Daddy are okay and so are we."

Sam was such a great daddy. That added affirmation to Kelly's decision to help him adopt the kids.

The girls finally stopped weeping when Kelly served the peaches with a package of cookies she'd brought from Europe for her parents.

"They might come in handy tonight," Arabella had said a few minutes ago as she'd handed the package to Kelly.

"Thanks, Mom." Kelly had been grateful that for once they seemed on the same page.

Smiles returned as everyone enjoyed the impromptu dessert and lasted right through the chores of cleanup.

"Mommy and Daddy would be so proud of you girls for helping like this," Kelly said when the last dish was put away. "Good job, guys."

The twins left happily to prepare for bed and another of Kelly's stories. Neil claimed he had a magazine he wanted to read and went upstairs, but Arabella paused in the kitchen doorway.

"If you would kindly inform me of which night you intend to schedule Sam's spaghetti dinner, your father and I will eat out," she said with disdain.

So much for harmony.

"Why would you do that, Mom?" Kelly asked curiously. "Don't you like spaghetti?"

"It's certainly not my favorite, but that's not the reason." Arabella let her gaze roam around the kitchen and landed on Sam with a glower. "If that's the kind of mess you created making a simple thing like tacos, I can just imagine the state of my daughter's kitchen when you get your hands on spaghetti sauce." After including Kelly in her scowl, she stomped upstairs.

Sam gaped after her for a moment then burst into laughter. He quickly slapped his hand over his mouth to stifle it.

Kelly had to do the same, shoulders shaking, though inside a part of her felt shame and sadness that her mother couldn't see tonight's meal for the success it had been.

"You see what you've created," Sam said when his broad shoulders finally stopped shaking. He glanced at the dishcloth he still held in his hand.

"That was not my fault," Kelly sputtered. His eyes searched hers, brimming with understanding. One of the girls came in for a kiss on a scratch. Kelly soothed the hurt, smiling as Emma danced away.

"I wish I knew how to do what you do," he said quietly. "It's a real gift."

"I didn't do anything special." Kelly stared, confused by his look of admiration.

"You turned a scratch into love. You made a chore— making supper—fun." Sam's smile transformed his handsome face into something Hollywood would long to capture. "You keep doing that, keep taking the responsibility I dump on you and making it an experience of learning that the kids can be part of it. Thank you."

"You're welcome." She arched one eyebrow. "But the learning experience was supposed to be for you, Sam, to help you build a repertoire of meals you can prepare for the twins when I'm gone."

For a moment he looked startled, then he laughed. "You continually surprise me, Kelly."

"I do?" She shoved her hair behind her ear so she could study him. "How?"

"You're very beautiful. You look like an open book with your innocent brown eyes," he told her. "But underneath, your brain is constantly working, isn't it? It's something I never noticed in Marina."

"Marina was more accepting of life than me." Kelly swallowed hard at the memories that cascaded. "She accepted what God sent her and worked with it. I'm not wired the same. I tend to stick my finger in the mix to help God out. As if He needs my help."

She rolled her eyes, meaning the remark to be light-hearted. But Sam didn't laugh. Instead he frowned, his brows drawing together in a glower.

"I think God does need help," he said in a brooding voice. "He needs help to see that people like Naomi don't deserve what He let her suffer. She lost everything that was precious to her."

"Did she lose your love?" Kelly watched his expression change, saw tenderness flood his face and thought how lucky his Naomi was to have experienced Sam's love.

"That could never happen," he said.

"Then she didn't lose everything. In fact, she had the most important thing a person can have in this life, and she had it right up until the day she died." Kelly knew he wouldn't like hearing it, but she had to say it anyway. "God gave you a love that stayed true."

"Yeah." A nerve flickered in his tightening jaw. "And then I buried her." He turned away, hiding his expression.

Kelly wasn't sure what to do next. She only knew that she had to somehow help him. Finally, she reached out and brushed her hand against his shoulder.

"I don't know the reason Naomi died, Sam. I don't know if you'll ever know why." She squeezed the tense muscles then let her fingers drop away. "But there was a reason. God doesn't just let things happen. Understanding His way isn't always possible. All you can do is trust that His way is best."

"That's *all* I can do?" He whirled around, his face tight with anger. "Somehow that doesn't comfort me very much. I can't think of one reason for a kind, compassionate God to let someone suffer, so excuse me if I'm having a little trouble with trusting." He tossed the towel on the counter and grabbed his jacket off a peg by the door. "I'm going to check on the newest calves. I'll be back before the kids go to bed."

Kelly watched him leave, her heart stinging at his words. Yet she knew that he spoke from pain and loss, because he couldn't reconcile his faith in God's goodness with Naomi's death.

"Help him," she prayed. "Please help him. Show me how to help him, too."

She was supposed to be here to help this family, but so far it seemed to Kelly that she wasn't doing a very good job.

Sam slammed down a bale of hay with a lot more force than necessary, furious with himself.

Why had he lashed out at Kelly like that? Naomi's suffering had nothing to do with her. Kelly certainly didn't owe him any explanations for her rock-solid faith. As Sam checked mothers and calves, Naomi's words, spoken through broken and chapped lips mere days before she'd passed away, returned to haunt him.

"God doesn't owe us any explanations, Sam." Her breathy voice had revealed the pain she'd tried so hard to hide from him. "We gave our lives to Him to do with as He wills, remember? I believe that He'll use my life. That's more important than anything, don't you think?"

"No," he snarled aloud, scaring the youngest calf, who ran away bawling for its mom.

Sam felt hemmed in, caught, snared like an unsuspecting rabbit. He stepped outside the barn, into the pasture, and glared at the sky, trying to release the pent-up anger he seldom allowed to vent. Until now.

Jake wasn't here to stop him or worry that he was losing it. The kids were inside with no idea their uncle was yelling at God. Kelly couldn't hear him, either. Even Oscar, his hired man, was off for the night. He was alone, and he needed to say what boiled inside him.

"You demand too much," he yelled at God. "I've waited. I hung on and tried to believe there was some purpose to her suffering. Nothing's changed. The world is no different. She's just another casualty of trusting You." His mouth tightened, but he had to say it. He couldn't keep it inside anymore. "*I* won't trust You ever again. I can't."

There was no flash of thunder to reprimand him; no blazing sword swooped down to lop off his head. No response at all, except that cold hard nub still lay buried deep inside him.

What was the point in railing like this? Either God couldn't hear or He didn't care. A relationship with God was supposed to be two-sided, but God was ignoring him.

Sam strode around the paddock, visually checking that the fence was secure so no wild animals could get near his herd. Satisfied, he let himself out through the gate then stood staring at the house, where his brother had built his family.

"I'll raise them the way Jake and Marina wanted," he promised softly, his breath emerging in puffs of vapor in the chilly night air. He needed to say this, to make his intent clear to God. "I'll take them to church on Sunday. I'll encourage them to be part of the congregation's activities. I'll do everything my brother would have done for them. But I'm not doing it for You. Do You understand? I'm doing it for *Jake*, because he trusted me and I intend to be worthy of his trust."

The light outside the back door flicked on, and the door opened. Kelly stood framed by the light streaming out behind her, peering into the darkness, arms wrapped around her middle to keep warm.

Was she worried about him?

The thought startled Sam. Why would she care about him? They were partners in looking out for the kids, but there was nothing personal between them.

And yet some inner part of Sam knew that wasn't quite true. He wanted, no, needed, to make sure she had everything she desired, that she wasn't suffering for coming here, for helping him. More than that, he wanted Kelly to like it on the Triple D—enough to stay?

But how could she? There was nothing for her here, nothing but a life as a glorified babysitter. Even if she did stay, when the twins and Jacob Samuel were finally old enough to leave home, Kelly's chance to further her career wouldn't exist.

The light disappeared as Kelly finally stepped inside the house and closed the door. A smile tugged at his lips. She was probably chilled from standing there so long. Now she'd likely go find that sweater she'd taken off earlier. He knew she wouldn't turn up the heat.

He was going to have to do something about Arabella. And he was going to start tomorrow morning. It was time for Arabella and Neil to move to their own place. Right after breakfast he'd talk with the Emersons, ask them about their house that Abby had spoken of.

Sam's thoughts returned to Kelly. Such a beautiful woman deserved to have a rich life with a husband who treasured her, to have children of her own to love, to fulfill the dreams he doubted she confided in others. Sam didn't expect a woman like her, who'd traveled the world, to be satisfied with a boring life on a cattle ranch outside Buffalo Gap, Alberta. It was silly to expect that.

But even in this short time, Sam had grown accustomed to seeing her pretty face when he went to the house. Now it seemed natural to seek her opinion about things, to heed her suggestions and to discuss plans for their parentless little family.

Everyone in Buffalo Gap and the surrounding district had expectations of Sam Denver. Two neighbors were after him to repair their balers. Another wanted his help with a motor for a well. He had his own stuff to ready for spring branding so they could move the herd north.

He was the guy who fixed things. At the moment, the weight of it all, the responsibility to his parents and the kids, felt like sacks of feed tied to his heels. He'd spent years longing to be free to travel anywhere for as long as he wanted.

Only now he didn't, even though he felt the weight of expectations. All Sam wanted now was for the twins to grow up happy and healthy. He wanted Jacob Samuel to know the kind of man his dad had been, to see what Jake had built with his hands. He wanted the twins to experience growing up on a ranch where you could run and jump and play without worry.

He wanted Kelly to see him as more than a dumb rancher who'd never been outside Canada or around anything other than a bunch of cattle.

Where did that come from?

As Sam mused on the peculiar thought intruding into his brain, he realized that though he'd known Kelly a very short time, he didn't feel any of the usual "shoulds" with her. *Should* figure out what she liked, *should* entertain her, *should* make things easier for her. From the moment she'd stepped onto the ranch, Kelly had fit in. She had her own interests, of course. Like that picture thing she was making from scraps of material. But her focus seemed primarily to rest on the kids and making their world right. She'd never given Sam the impression that she looked down on him, son of a rancher, nondescript and boring.

In fact, the two of them seemed to click on most subjects. Except God.

When Kelly Krause looked at him, Sam hoped she saw someone she could trust, someone she felt comfortable sharing with. She treated him as more than just the acting head of the family. She treated him like a close friend.

Sam liked that about Kelly. He liked it a lot.

Actually, he liked too much about Kelly. If he wasn't careful, something could start building between them.

Start? his brain mocked.

"Okay," he acknowledged out loud to the frosted world around him. He sighed, his breath forming a huge white cloud that seemed to hang in the air. "I admit we have some kind of connection. But nothing's going to happen, because I won't let it."

He trudged back toward the house, knowing the kids would be waiting for him to kiss them good-night. He paused at the door to gaze up into the starry night and remembered an Eskimo saying Oscar had told him about.

Maybe those aren't stars in the sky. Maybe they are the eyes of our loved ones, watching us.

Jake? Are you there? I miss you.

The cry of a coyote echoing through the air broke the quietness and dragged Sam back to reality. He stepped inside the porch and shrugged off his coat and boots as the sounds and smells of what had become home carried to him. Kids' bathtime, a baby's murmur and giggles. He walked eagerly toward the bedrooms. It wasn't so bad, this fatherhood thing. It wasn't bad at all.

The bad part was yet to come. Just when they'd all become accustomed to Kelly making their lives so sweet, she'd leave.

And then Sam would be left to manage all on his own. The empty hole in his heart yawned a little wider as he dredged up a smile and walked into the kids' bedrooms to say good-night.

"Don't put that there, Kelly. Can't you see it's out of place?"

Saturday, two weeks later, Sam winced. Arabella moved around her new home as she continued nagging her daughter about everything from the correct placement of her beloved dishes in the Emersons' china cabinets to how to place magazines on the built-in shelves at a precise forty-five-degree angle.

Two hours ago he'd been amused by how quickly the movers had departed Buffalo Gap after emptying their truck of the Krause belongings and loading them into the Emersons' former home. Now Sam wished he'd left with them.

"Kelly, don't you have any taste? This isn't a gaudy cruise ship, you know."

As Arabella snatched the lamp from her daughter's hand and placed it in exactly the same spot Kelly had put it ten minutes earlier, Sam decided he'd had enough. He took out his phone and called Mayor Marsha to beg for her help. Then he deliberately dropped the hassock he was carrying, hearing its thump with some satisfaction.

"Sam!" Arabella hurried over to inspect, as if he'd made a dent in the very thick carpet. "We're not throwing around cattle here."

"I've lifted cows that didn't weigh as much as that thing," he grumbled. "Is it in the right place now, or should I move it over there?" He curled his fingers around the cushion top, pretending he was going to pull it by that.

"No, no." A horrified Arabella placed her hand on his. "It's fine here. Thank you. Thank you so much for your help. You've done so much by finding us this place and helping us get situated. We truly appreciate it." She stepped protectively between him and her other furniture as she spoke.

"I like this chair," Neil said and immediately sank into the comfy arms of a leather recliner. "I've always liked this chair." He held out a hand to Kelly. "You used to call it 'the daddy chair,'" he said with a little smile.

"That wasn't this cha—"

"Why did you call it that, Kelly?" Sam interrupted Arabella before she could point out Neil's mistake. Didn't she know that correcting him all the time only made him more frustrated?

"I think it had something to do with a story Dad used to tell me," Kelly murmured. She laced her fingers in her father's then bent over and brushed a kiss against his cheek.

"You were always late getting to bed when he read it," Arabella snapped. "And all worked up." Her gaze strayed to Kelly's hand enfolding her dad's. "It wasn't even a child's story," she said in her sour tone. "I don't know where he got it from."

"Didn't matter." Kelly's voice lost the nostalgia. "I loved it. Do you still have it?"

"No." Arabella's eyes glittered with triumph. "I had to throw it out. It was tattered." Sam suspected she'd done it deliberately.

"No." Neil dug in the side pocket of his chair and pulled out a jumble of pages. "I saved it, Kelly."

"Dad! Thank you. May I keep it? Maybe I can get it fixed?" She held out her hand and after a sideways look at his wife, Neil gave her the book.

"Keep it," he said softly. "For your kids."

Sam's throat blocked at the look that passed between father and daughter, a look that said *I understand.*

"Kelly doesn't have any children, remember, Neil?" Arabella's harsh voice echoed around the room. "Kelly ran aw—"

"Could we stop for a break now?" Sam asked loudly. "I could sure use a cup of coffee."

"But I don't want to stop now. I want to arrange things the way I like them," Arabella protested. "Anyway, I haven't yet unpacked my coffeemaker."

"Oh." The doorbell rang. Sam almost grinned at the open opportunity. "You have guests. It would probably be

better if we got out of your way because we don't seem to
know how you want things. Kelly, Neil, why don't we leave
Arabella to her company while we get a coffee? We'll bring
one back for you," he promised, smothering a chuckle at the
glare she shot his way as she walked to the door.

"Mayor Marsha," she enthused, suddenly all smiles.
"Come in."

"Come on, guys," Sam chided in a low voice. "Get your
coats."

"Good idea. You two have a visit. We'll get out of your
way." Kelly hurried to lift their coats from the front hall
closet. "You want coffee, Dad, or something else?"

"A milkshake," he said loudly. "A strawberry milkshake.
I haven't had one since you and I went roller-skating."

"Roller-skating? I think I was ten." Kelly chuckled at
the memory.

Sam held the coats, allowing first Kelly then her father
to slide their arms into the sleeves. Then he shrugged into
his own sheepskin-lined jacket.

"See you, Mayor. We won't be long," he promised Arabella. "If you need anything moved, wait till we come back
and I'll do it. Okay?" He didn't wait for her agreement before pulling open the front door. "Let's go."

A few minutes later the three of them were seated in the
diner, waiting for two coffees, a strawberry milkshake and
a big plate of French fries.

"I'm sure glad to see you, Kelly. You were gone a long
time." Neil smiled happily at his daughter.

"I missed you, too, Dad." Kelly laced her fingers with
his then grinned at Sam. "Isn't this fun?"

Everything was fun with Kelly, Sam thought, but he
didn't say that aloud. He guessed she'd probably never
walked out on her mom before, but he wasn't sorry he'd
arranged it, because now father and daughter were happily
chatting, smiling as they drank and remembered the past.

Neil, it seemed, loved French fries and after drowning them in ketchup, managed to eat almost the entire plate. Sam was glad this was one of his days of clarity.

When they dropped off Neil an hour or so later, Marsha was still there. Arabella sat across from her, face wreathed in smiles. Kelly set down Arabella's coffee and a bag with two tarts inside.

"I thought you might like something with your coffee, though I guess we're a little late," she said.

"These little towns often don't have the best bakeries." Arabella must have realized she'd offended Marsha, because she backtracked fast. "But I've heard Buffalo Gap's is one of the best. Thank you."

"You're welcome." Kelly looked stunned. "Well, we've got to get back to the ranch now. Maybe you should leave whatever still needs doing till tomorrow, Mom. I imagine you're tired."

"Oh, Marsha helped me finish what needs to be done now. The rest can wait. We're just discussing quilting. Marsha and I share the interest." Arabella waggled her fingers. "Good night." She ushered them out and firmly closed her new front door behind them.

Sam blinked, noticed Kelly also appeared shocked.

"Where has that woman been and why didn't someone introduce her to my mother before?" she whispered.

"Don't question a good thing." He deliberately neglected to tell her he'd made the call. "You might not have noticed, but we're having that chinook you wanted," he teased. He took her arm to guide her around melting ice puddles and into the truck.

"I did notice and I love it." She unzipped her jacket. "Maybe soon I won't need this."

"I wouldn't toss it just yet," Sam warned. "The Weather Channel says we're to get freezing rain tonight, turning to snow tomorrow." He chuckled at her groan. "You gotta toughen up, girl."

"Yeah." She shuddered and zipped up her coat again.

"I suggest we stock up on groceries then head home before the slush freezes," Sam said. "Do you think your parents need anything?"

"Mom told me earlier that she'd phoned for a grocery delivery, so I think they're fine," Kelly told him. "But thanks for thinking of them."

"No problem. So we'll stock up and then head home to rescue my mother from the kids. By now she probably needs it," Sam teased.

But Kelly didn't laugh.

"I appreciate everything you did today, Sam." Kelly's brown eyes met his. "I know it hasn't been easy, having my mom criticizing all the time. I can't imagine how you finally persuaded her to move, but I'm very aware that she has tested everyone's patience."

"Whatever I did was for you." Sam chuckled at her wide-eyed surprise. "She was wearing you out with her critical attitude. I figured that if you were going to handle the kids, you needed some space. I'll do whatever it takes to support you and make it easier on you, Kelly." He paused. "That's why I happened to mention to your mom that our local quilter's group is competing with one in Calgary. I knew she couldn't resist joining."

"Having her speak to Hilda Cramer before they moved was a good idea, too. I think she feels much happier about the move, knowing Hilda can help care for Dad. Added to which, Mom will have a sewing room again. That means a lot." Kelly sighed. "I don't know how to thank you, Sam."

"Pie?" he suggested slyly. Kelly rolled her eyes.

Inside the store they filled two carts with items from Kelly's list. He had to laugh when she lifted an apple pie from the shelf.

"Perhaps the local bakery isn't up to my mother's standards, but will it meet yours?" Kelly asked tongue-in-cheek.

"Absolutely." As they waited in line at the checkout, Sam thought again how different it was to shop with Kelly. More fun.

He fell to thinking of all the fun times they'd shared and only blinked back to awareness when Kelly nudged him.

"Wake up. Sheena's here."

"Let him sleep. I'm told men as old as Sam need a rest in the afternoon," the travel agent teased.

"Hey!" he protested as Kelly hooted with laughter.

"How about getting together?" Sheena asked Kelly. "We haven't managed that yet and I really want to."

"Why don't you come out to the ranch tomorrow after church?" Sam suggested. "I'm making chili."

"*You're* making chili—" Sheena stared at him, eyes wide. She knew he never touched a stove unless it was to heat a can of soup.

Sam tried to quell his flush of satisfaction at her surprise and finally her agreement to join them for lunch. As he loaded the groceries, he didn't even try to pretend he wasn't feeling pretty smug about the whole cooking thing.

"Dad seemed almost like his old self today," Kelly mused as they drove to the ranch.

"Physically he's very fit." Sam gave voice to an idea he'd tossed around. "I think we should pick him up some afternoon when we take the kids sliding down my favorite hill on my old sled. Neil might enjoy going along to watch." He paused then added, "We could have French fries afterward. He certainly seems to enjoy those. At least, he sure wasn't big on sharing."

Sam managed to keep a straight face when Kelly glanced at him.

"Oh, poor baby. Were you starving? Again?" She doubled over with laughter at his hard-done-by look.

"I worked hard for your mom," he said defensively. "He ate almost all those fries."

"At least there's nothing wrong with Dad's appetite," she agreed. Her gaze dropped to the book from her childhood she'd placed on the seat between them.

Sam only realized when he pulled into the yard that tears filled her eyes. "What's wrong?" he asked, hating the helpless feeling her weeping brought.

"I'm beginning to realize what I'll miss when I leave." Kelly touched the book reverently then lifted her head to stare at him. "He'll never be able to tell my kids that story, if I had any. And how many more times will I get to hear him laugh like that? Bit by bit this disease is stealing my father."

Kelly's sobs sounded as if her heart was breaking. And that tender, gentle heart of hers probably was. Sam shoved the gearshift into Park, set her book on the dash then leaned over and drew her into his embrace, sliding his hand down her back in what he hoped would soothe her enough to stop those sobs. His comforting her and her trying to help him over the hard spots was happening more and more often. It was good to have someone to share with again.

"There's only one thing you can do," he told her when her tears finally ceased.

"What's that?" Kelly peered at him through lashes stuck together by her tears.

"Love him the very best you can now." Sam eased a few damp strands of hair away from her lips. Even crying, with her face mottled, Kelly Krause was gorgeous. "That's what I'm learning from Jake's death. Cherish each moment together. You don't know if you'll get another."

"It's good advice," Kelly agreed. "Thank you, Sam." She nestled against his chest, resting there. After a few moments she gave a huge sigh. "I seem to keep bawling all over you."

"I like it," Sam said, only realizing the truth as he said it.

"Someday you have to tell me how a beautiful woman like you doesn't have a boyfriend insisting you get back to him."

A sad little smile twisted her lips. "How do you know I don't?"

"Do you?" Stunned by the strength of his opposition to that thought, Sam leaned back to look into her eyes. "But you never seem to get any mail—oh, of course. Email. I'm sure he misses you very much."

"Afraid not." Kelly drew back. "There's no one, Sam. Not anymore."

Not anymore? "Because?" He wanted to know so badly.

"He went back to his first love. I couldn't compete with the history they had together." She sighed then shook her head. "Don't say you're sorry, because it was the right thing to happen. It took having my heart broken and a trip to Israel before I was ready to accept that God's plans for me don't include marriage. It's taking me a while, but I'm growing to accept His will."

No! Every cell in Sam's body protested those words. Kelly was chock-full of love, just waiting to shower it over someone. She was the kind of woman whose heart gave and gave. She couldn't stay alone for the rest of her life. It would be a terrible waste when she had so much to give. But he couldn't say that. It would only make her feel worse.

Sam searched for a different way to comfort her but all he could come up with was, "Don't worry about the future, Kelly. We'll get through things together."

"Until I have to go." Her big brown eyes searched his through the twilight shadows of the dash lights. "I wish I could stay here, Sam. I truly do."

"So stay." *Please?* The intensity of his desire for her to stay shocked him as he realized he hadn't been thinking only about the kids. *He* wanted her to stay.

"I can't stay, Sam. What would I do? There are no cruise ships, no ports. I don't know anything about small towns and even less about ranching." She cupped his cheek in her palm. "You've been so kind, so generous, to me and my family. I wish I could watch the twins and Jacob Samuel grow up. I wish I could be here to spend more time with my dad, but that isn't going to happen. Sooner or later I have to go back to my life. So I guess you're right. I'll cherish every moment that I'm here." She smiled at him. "Starting now. Shall we go in?"

Sam nodded but as he walked beside Kelly up the path, his arms full of grocery bags, he realized that in the short time she'd been here, he'd grown accustomed to hearing her perspective and sharing ideas. More than that, he valued her opinion.

He'd also seen just how the years apart had left her yearning for her father and wondered why she hadn't come home earlier. Not that it mattered. She was here now and could savor the moments with him while he could still share them. Yet part of Sam ached to make it better for Kelly.

Can't You fix this? he asked God. *Can't I?*

The answer circled round and round inside Sam's head. *How?*

Chapter Seven

"I never imagined Sam could actually cook something," Sheena marveled, nursing her cup of tea at the kitchen table with Kelly. They turned together to look out the window at the twins chasing Sam through the puddles dotted around the yard. "My sister would have loved to see that."

"Oh." Not understanding her meaning, Kelly glanced outside, relieved that the forecasted snow had been changed to light rain, even though it meant that she'd be doing more laundry tonight. "Have I met her?"

"My older sister was Sam's fiancée," Sheena explained. "Naomi."

"Oh. I didn't know." Kelly covered Sheena's hand with her own.

"Of course you didn't. Naomi died three years ago. I still miss her a lot. I'm sure you know the feeling." She smiled when Kelly nodded soberly.

"Tell me about her," Kelly invited, curious about the woman Sam had loved.

"Naomi was my business partner, but she had a lot more travel knowledge than I do." Sheena smiled as she reminisced. "She started traveling as an exchange student in high school. She was in France for a year, and her host family traveled a lot so she saw most of Europe with people who knew the area."

"With a local is always the best way to see a foreign place." Kelly's brain swirled with questions about Sam's beloved fiancée.

"Naomi took her training then worked for a big agency in Calgary. I'd always been entranced by her travel stories, so when I finished school, I took the same training. Before I finished, our parents died. Naomi decided to move back to Buffalo Gap and set up an agency. We became partners and it worked very well." Sheena sighed. "She died before we could realize her dream to expand our business."

"You still have time," Kelly soothed.

"Maybe. The internet is encroaching more and more." Sheena leaned forward, her face serious. "Naomi and Sam intended to organize tours overseas, escorted vacations from Buffalo Gap."

"That's a great idea. Lots of people enjoy having their trip organized so that all they have to do is sit back and enjoy." She sat back and waited, wondering why Sheena hadn't pursued her sister's idea.

"I'd like to do that." The light in her bright eyes faded. "My problem is that I never traveled like Naomi did. I don't know enough to organize tours, let alone lead them. And I'd need someone to cover for me in the office while I'm away."

"How can I help you?" Kelly asked, touched by Sheena's plight. This sprightly woman with her obvious zest for life would make a wonderful tour leader.

"I haven't got all the problems worked out yet. I'm trusting God to help me solve those." Sheena grinned. "But I was hoping you could give me some tips on how to get started organizing my first tour group to Australia. I have plenty of senior clients who want to go, but it's a long way and they don't want to travel alone."

Kelly nodded, her brain busy.

"Is it too much to ask?" Sheena worried.

"Of course not. I have a few ideas," Kelly said. "If you want them."

"I do." Sheena grinned. "I knew from the way Marina talked that you'd be willing to help me. Your sister bragged on you all the time."

"Really?" Kelly stared at her.

"Uh-huh." Sheena nodded. "She told me several times that I should take a trip on one of your ships. That's what she and Jake planned to do before the twins and Jacob Samuel came."

"I wish she had," Kelly murmured. How she would have loved to show her sister her world. All she could do now was honor her memory. Helping Sheena seemed the perfect way.

"Maybe I shouldn't have bothered you," Sheena said, eyes downcast.

"Are you kidding?" Kelly grinned. "I love the ranch, but travel has been my life for almost ten years. I love to talk about it with someone who's interested. Here's my thought. First go on a cruise yourself, one that visits some of the highlights where you could take your tour in Australia. That will give you an overview of the kind of things your guests will see. Go on the shore excursions, take tons of pictures and make lots of notes."

"Okay." Sheena scribbled madly on her notepad.

"You might even want to make a cruise part of the tour you're planning." She kept throwing out ideas, pausing every so often so Sheena could keep up.

Kelly was prepared for the familiar yen for adventure to grab hold while she was talking. But when her glance lifted to the window where Sam and the girls were trying to build a snow fort, she realized that she didn't want to go anywhere. She was perfectly happy right here, caring for the children and doing what she could to help solidify Sam's case for fatherhood.

As she waved an ecstatic Sheena goodbye a half hour later, Kelly glanced at Sam. A glow of warmth suffused her. She actually loved this life. No wonder Marina had been happy here. She'd found everything she most cared about on the Triple D.

Bemused by the satisfaction she now felt, Kelly pulled out ingredients to make an apple pie. But before she could begin, the phone rang. It was Abby from Family Ties Adoption Agency.

"Hi, Abby. How are you?" she asked cheerfully.

"Fine, thanks." A pause. "Kelly, I need to talk to you and Sam. Now. Can I come over?"

Fear tiptoed up Kelly's spine. Abby wanted to talk now, on Sunday? Something was wrong.

"Kelly?"

"Yes, I'm here. But Sam's outside with the girls." She thought for a moment. They couldn't keep calling his mother to help any more than her mother could keep calling them. "Come on over, Abby. I'll set up something to keep the twins busy while we talk."

"I'll be there in fifteen minutes." Abby hung up.

Kelly stared at her pie ingredients. Her gaze lifted to the window where Sam was dusting off the snowy twins. They'd come in soon. She plugged in the kettle to make cocoa then decided pie making could come later. Instead, she stirred together a batch of play dough. By the time the three chilled fort builders came inside, Kelly had mugs of cocoa and yesterday's peanut butter cookies waiting.

"We had fun." Sam's cheeks flushed bright from the cool air. He helped the twins shed their gear. "It's a gorgeous day, Kelly. I'll stay with the kids if you want to go for a walk."

"Maybe later I'll do that," she said, thrilled that he'd

thought of her. "Girls, you need to change out of those wet things. After you do that and wash your hands, you can have a snack." Kelly waited till they'd raced away before facing Sam. "Abby's on her way over. She needs to talk to us."

His face tightened. The joy that had brightened his green eyes a moment earlier snuffed out as shadows crept in. "What now?"

"I don't know." Kelly put her hand on his when he picked up the phone receiver. "I don't want to bother your mom today. I have something for the girls to do in here while we talk in the dining room."

Sam's countenance lifted a little. "Thank you, Kelly. I appreciate your thoughtfulness, and I know my mother does, too."

"No problem." She enjoyed the way their styles meshed as he got the girls settled at the table for their snack while she changed Jacob Samuel. She handed the baby to Sam to feed before starting a pot of coffee to brew. "We might need this," she murmured for Sam's ears only. "Though I'm praying otherwise."

Sam's lips tightened at her words, but he didn't say anything. Maybe because just then Abby's car pulled into the yard.

Once the excited twins had greeted her and reveled in her praise for their fort, Sam, with Jacob Samuel in his arms, led Abby into the dining room to enjoy their coffee. Kelly could hear the baby's gurgle and their low voices chatting as she showed the twins the play dough and cutters.

"You two call if you need help," Kelly said. "But I don't want you to come into the dining room."

"'Cause this is messy." Sadie held up a long sausage of dough with bits falling.

"Messy," Emma repeated in her soft voice. "We'll stay here," she promised.

"Thank you, sweetheart. You two are the best." Kelly kissed the top of each head then carried her coffee into the dining room. "We haven't seen you for a while, Abby."

"We've had a rash of deliveries at Family Ties," Abby said with a smile. "I've been acting like a stork, delivering babies to their new parents."

"That must be fun." Kelly sat down with Sam on her left. For some reason it felt better to have him within reach.

"Fun for sure, but it means I get behind on office correspondence. Like this. It came last week when I was out of the office." Abby selected a paper from her bag and held it out toward Sam. "I've been notified that Eunice Edwards had an assessment done on herself, her husband and their home. She's not waiting, Sam. She's going ahead full steam with her claim to adopt the twins."

"The result?" Sam, face inscrutable, ignored the paper she held to study the baby in his high chair.

"Very favorable," Abby said quietly. "She was rated on extremely high standards and passed them all with flying colors."

Kelly glanced from her to Sam, worried by both their silences. "So what do we do now?" she asked when no one said anything.

"Pray?" Abby suggested.

"You're saying Sam's case hasn't got a ghost of a chance?" she pressed, needing to fully understand the ramifications of Abby's visit.

"No. Sam's strongest card was always that he was younger and you're younger, meaning more fit, closer to the twins' ages, maybe better suited to raising a child than this older aunt." Abby let the paper drift to the table. "But Sam's a single man. With this report…" She paused, shook her head. "It's going to be much harder than I anticipated to persuade a judge that the twins are better off here on the Triple D with Sam."

"There has to be something we can do." Kelly could hardly breathe for the heaviness on her heart. The twins belonged with Sam. After spending six weeks at the Triple D, she was more certain of that than she'd ever been. She saw a flicker in Abby's steady gaze that gave her hope. "Tell us what it is," she begged, desperate to stop this, even as her brain shot a thousand prayers upward.

"Sam's chances of adopting the girls would go up astronomically if he was married." Abby's words hit like stones in a pond, sending out shock waves that made both Sam and Kelly gape at her.

"Not going to happen," Sam said flatly after a moment's pause. "My fiancée died, remember?"

"I know, but I thought maybe—" After a quick glance at Kelly, Abby cut off whatever she'd been about to say and shook her head. "Never mind that. What we have to do now is build the strongest case we can. We still have the fact that the girls consider this their home in our favor. That could count for a lot."

"Sure." Sam pushed back from the table, his face hard as chiseled stone. "Thank you for telling us, Abby. We'll do what we can but truthfully, I doubt it'll be enough."

"Sam, you can't give up." Kelly lowered her voice. "Jake and Marina chose you to be the twins' father. There has to be a way to make it happen."

"How?" he demanded. "Tell me and I'll do it."

Kelly could think of only one way. "We need to pray."

One corner of his lovely mouth lifted in a sneer.

"Because that's worked so well." Sam's voice revealed his bitter disappointment. He folded the paper and tucked it in his pocket. "I'm sorry to interrupt your Sunday afternoon, Abby. Keep in touch." Then he left.

"I'm sorry." Kelly's heart ached for this man who'd done everything he could to honor his brother's wishes. "He's re-

ally hurting. He loves the twins so much. To lose them—"
She couldn't say the unthinkable.

"We haven't lost them yet," Abby said sternly. "You're
going to have to help Sam refocus on what he needs to do
to firm up his case. Get the loose ends dealt with so there's
nothing to question, nothing to suggest a future problem."
She rose.

"I've been pushing him to get the paperwork in order,"
Kelly told her. "Understandably, it hasn't been a priority
for Sam because he's doing his best to be all things to all
people."

"As are you." Abby touched her arm, her smile sympa-
thetic. "I know it isn't easy, but if you can keep things on
an even keel for all of them, I think everyone will feel more
secure. You're an amazing helper for Sam. Keep praying. I
will, too, and I'll alert the prayer chain at church. We need
some heavy petitioning of God to work this out."

"Thank you, Abby. We appreciate your help so much,
even if Sam didn't say it." Kelly tried to smile but couldn't.
Her heart was just too heavy at the thought of him losing his precious twins. She lifted Jacob Samuel into her
arms, needing the soft warmth of his little body to cheer
her. "It's up to God to work out," she murmured into the
baby's wispy hair.

"I've been studying Deuteronomy in my devotions,"
Abby said thoughtfully. "One verse keeps coming back to
me. It's in the seventh chapter. 'Know therefore that the
Lord your God is God; He is the faithful God, keeping His
covenant of love to a thousand generations of those who
love Him and keep His commands.'" She smiled gently.
"Focus on that promise, Kelly. It may be that this circum-
stance is God's way of bringing Sam back to Himself."

"I hope so." Her heart weary, Kelly walked with Abby
to the door and hugged her. "Thank you again," she whis-

pered just before Abby left. Kelly turned to find the twins studying her with frowns.

"What's wrong with Uncle Sam?" Sadie asked.

"He didn't want to play with us," Emma whispered.

"He's got a lot of work to do." She studied the two precious faces and decided to make today a special day. Because it was. They were all together, though who knew for how long. "Would you like to help me make Uncle Sam an apple pie?"

With ecstatic agreement and a quick cleanup of the play dough, the kitchen was soon ready for baking. These past weeks Kelly had found comfort in putting together sweet treats for her little "family." Today she wanted to make something special for Sam, to show him they were together in this.

Making a pie took much longer than Kelly had anticipated, thanks to the twins' helping hands. But they had so much fun, she decided to also mix a batch of fresh rolls for dinner.

"Does God like food?" Sadie paused in her effort to mold a hunk of overworked bun dough into crescents.

"I do." Emma grinned at them then returned to the soapy dishes she was scrubbing.

"He must," Sadie said with tightly furrowed brow.

"Why?" Kelly asked curiously.

"'Cause Oscar tole me the Bible says God made everything an' it was good." Sadie thumped and prodded the last bit of dough. "More flour, please."

"Just a tiny bit more." Kelly dusted a bit of powder over the dough then lifted it to join the other rolls. "We have to let it rise now," she said to a protesting Sadie. "Otherwise, it won't be ready in time for supper."

"Okay." Sadie tugged at her apron. "I'll play with my dolls."

"Me, too." Emma rinsed her hands then held out her arms.

"Thank you both for your help, darlings." Kelly slid off their aprons then pressed a kiss to the top of each blond head as she lifted them from their stools.

Sadie leaned over to kiss Jacob Samuel's cheek then grinned. "My Sunday school teacher said I'm Jacob Samuel's big sister an' I should love him lots."

"She was absolutely right," Kelly managed to squeeze out around the lump in her throat. *They're a family, God. Please don't let that be broken.*

Something made her turn. Sam stood in the doorway, his lean body slumped, his face gaunt and gray, his eyes totally empty of their sparkle.

"You and Emma are Jacob Samuel's sisters," Kelly said firmly, keeping her gaze fixed on Sam. "You're his family."

"I love my fam'ly an' I love you and my uncle Sam," Sadie crooned. She pressed her cheek against Sam's leg for a moment then skipped down the hall to find her dolls. Emma blew them a kiss then raced after her sister.

Sam held Kelly's gaze for a long time before he finally cleared his throat. "I need a refill before I get back to my work in the study," he mumbled. He filled his mug with coffee then disappeared.

Kelly longed to follow him, to offer to help, to be there in case he needed her. And then she wondered.

Who would comfort Sam when she was gone?

That troublesome thought wouldn't leave her for the rest of the day.

Sam loved Kelly's video nights. Ever since she'd discovered Marina's massive collection of recorded events, Kelly had spent painstaking hours organizing them chronologically. As March gave way to spring's tentative arrival, she would insist they gather periodically for an evening or an inclement afternoon to view some particular family event Marina had proudly recorded.

For those few moments Sam could sit back, savor the sound of Jake's hearty laugh and his overwhelming love for his wife and pretend everything was all right in his world. For a few moments he could let go of the mind-numbing fear that he was going to lose the twins.

Sam worried at first that these times might become maudlin. Instead, the short segments were now happily anticipated events when the girls remembered their parents, mostly with giggles and joy. It was the only time when Emma seemed to truly relax, and Sam kept hoping that small sign of progress would increase. If he could just be patient.

"That's when we first came to live here. I look funny, don't I?" Sadie tilted her head to one side, studying her on-screen image.

"Your hair does look a bit odd." Kelly compared the video to the wild disarray of curls on Sadie's head. "You cut it, didn't you?" Sadie nodded. "By yourself?"

"Uh-huh. A boy, Thomas, said my hair made me blind like that guy in the Bible. Bart—somebody. So I cutted it." Sadie shrugged. "Thomas laughed at me."

"You didn't mind him laughing at you?" Sam glanced from her to Emma, noting the quick look between them and the smug smile on Emma's face. "How come?"

"'Cause Emma fixed him." Sadie's grin spread across her entire face.

"Emma *fixed* him?" Sam sat up, suddenly alert, hoping this was only another of the fantastic stories Sadie had recently begun concocting. He glanced at Kelly but her face reflected her puzzlement. "How did Emma *fix* him, Sadie Lady?"

"Socked him." Emma's plain two-word answer shocked Sam. Apparently, it had the same effect on Kelly. After a moment of silence she licked her lips.

"Uh, you hit—?" She stopped, frowned then glanced at him, a question in her eyes.

Sam knew exactly what she was thinking. How exactly did one reprimand a child for defending her twin? He noticed Emma shifting nearer to Sadie.

"With your fist?" Why hadn't he heard anything about this?

"With a puppet. It had a hard head." Sadie looked at Emma. "Thomas cried."

Sam felt struck dumb. Sweet little Emma?

"Sweetie, where did this happen?" Kelly asked in a careful voice.

"At Sunday school." Both twins nodded. "That boy's mommy said we were—" Sadie frowned then shrugged. "I dunno. But it wasn't nice so we didn't go no more."

"But honey," Kelly said with a frown, "you go to Sunday school every week."

"I tole you." Sadie sighed. "That was before we came here. When we lived at 'nother house."

"A different Sunday school," Emma clarified in her soft voice. "It wasn't nice like ours."

"I see." Sam looked at Kelly, hoping she had some notion of how to deal with this information, because he certainly didn't.

"Girls, um, it's not nice to hit people because they laugh at you." Kelly waited then lifted an eyebrow at Sam as if she expected him to add something.

"Don't do it again, okay?" He couldn't compute the image of Emma doffing some older kid.

"That's what our mommy said." Sadie glanced at the screen, which had gone blank, then to the window. "It's raining again."

"April showers bring May flowers," Emma parroted.

"Your birthdays are in May." The sudden memory made Sam tense, even more at Sadie's next question.

"When are we gonna have our party?" She turned to Emma. "I'll be five, so I can invite five people. So can Emma."

Ten kids racing around, wanting to be entertained? Sam struggled to breathe and wondered if this nauseous feeling was the start of a heart attack. He glanced at Kelly, who didn't look worried at all. In fact, she was smiling.

"Let's make a list." She got a pad of paper and a pen and kneeled so she could use the coffee table to write on. The twins plopped down on either side of her. "What kind of birthday cake would you like?"

"Pink." Sadie threw Emma a look. "Right?"

Emma shook her head, curls bobbling. "Choc'late," she whispered.

Sam couldn't tear his gaze from Kelly, marveling at her easy approach to something he'd been dreading. Was his mother right? Had God played a part in leading her here?

"That means two cakes, or at least two layers. What would you like to do for your birthday?" She caught him studying her and tilted her head to one side as she asked, "What do kids do for parties in Buffalo Gap, Sam?"

As if he knew.

"I want a treasure hunt an' a gold chest with money candy." Sadie inhaled then added, "And balloons."

"Hm. A treasure hunt could be fun." Kelly looked at Emma. "What would you like to do on your birthday, sweetie?"

"Fishin'." Emma stuffed her knuckles into her mouth and hung her head.

"Anything else?" Kelly prodded, but Emma only shook her head and remained silent.

Sam tried to catch Kelly's eye and when he did, he shook his head vehemently. No way was he taking ten, no, twelve kids down by the river with spring runoff so high. Kelly ignored him.

"When are your birthdays?" she asked. When neither child answered, she glanced at him. "Sam?"

Now she wanted to hear from him? "May 15th."

"We're havin' a treasure hunt." Sadie danced from one foot to the other.

"No, fishin'," Emma said then fell silent at Sadie's glare.

"Uncle Sam and I need some time to think about it, okay?" Kelly rose. "It's bedtime now, girls."

Sadie started to groan until Kelly tapped her birthday list with her pen. The little girl swallowed, turned and headed for the bathroom, Emma trailing behind.

"I wish I'd said their birthdays were in November," Sam grumbled, trying to smother his laughter. "Could have enjoyed early bedtime for months while they hoped for their party." He rose and picked up the baby from his swing chair. "By the way, there will be no fishing."

Kelly turned away, saying merely, "We'll see."

"No, Kelly, I mean it," he said more sternly. "The water's running fast and it's high. It would be crazy to take little kids near it. They'd drown."

"Oh, good grief." Kelly whirled around, brown eyes snapping. Sam automatically took a step back at the anger she radiated, but she moved forward and stood toe-to-toe. "I never took you for a wet blanket, Sam."

That made him mad.

"Maybe you don't understand," he snapped, juggling Jacob Samuel from one hip to the other while he strove to keep his voice even. "I'm responsible for the twins and him. I can't let them be in danger for a mere birthday party."

"A *mere* birthday party." Her brown eyes sparked as she glared at him. "It's their fifth birthday, Sam, and the first one without their parents."

"So we'll celebrate with something other than fishing. Emma will understand." Frustration nipped him when Kelly's jaw tightened.

"I don't want that sweet little girl to *understand*," she said, enunciating each word in a harsh yet soft voice. "I want her to laugh so hard she can't stop. I want her to forget whatever's bothering her and speak clearly and plainly. I want Sadie to shiver with excitement when she goes on her treasure hunt. Don't you?"

"I don't want them hurt." He stood firm.

"And I do?" Kelly studied him for a long time before she finally sighed. "There are ways to have a fishing pond that won't hurt anyone." She shook her head when he didn't speak. "It's always black-and-white with you, isn't it, Sam?"

"I don't know what you mean." But he thought from the way Kelly was glaring at him that he was going to find out.

"God's bad because Naomi died. He must be insensitive and cruel to have allowed such a thing. Emma can't possibly fish on her birthday because someone's sure to fall in the river and drown and you'll be blamed. You can't adopt the twins because there's a great-aunt with a sterling reputation who wants them and so, of course, she'll win custody." Her voice dropped at the sounds of the twins returning. "Where's your faith, Sam? Why can't you open your heart and mind so God can fill it with possibilities?"

"Because every time I do, I get slapped down," he snapped in a low voice.

"Everybody has problems. But we get up, dust ourselves off and try again." She reached up and cupped his cheek. "It's called life, and you can't ever, ever give up." Her eyes had lost their fire now, and something soft and warm filled them. "Live in the possibilities, Sam. Let go of the past."

Jacob Samuel wiggled in Sam's arms, but he couldn't move. For a moment, a fraction of a nanosecond, as Kelly's gaze held his, Sam thought he glimpsed the future. The kids were there. So was Kelly.

And then reality intruded.

"Are we havin' a story?" Sadie asked.

"Of course we are." Kelly's hand slid from his face. She turned away, sat on the sofa so the twins could hug near her on either side. "Tonight the princess's lovely boat lands in a new place."

"What's it called?" Emma whispered.

"The Town of Possibility." Kelly lifted her head and stared at him. "It's called Possibility because no one can even imagine the wonderful things that are waiting there."

Before Sam got caught in the fantasy world, he left. He changed Jacob Samuel one last time then snuggled him into his crib and set the musical mobile moving. He stood there, watching the little boy settle to sleep. His gaze fell on the picture on the far wall.

Three things endure. Faith, hope and love.

Sam loved the kids, no question. What he lacked was faith and hope for their futures. Or rather, he was losing it because of all the problems that kept piling on, not the least of which were the income tax papers he still hadn't filed.

Kelly was right. He had stopped dreaming, stopped imagining, stopped hoping, not just for the kids but for himself and his future. He couldn't see past the obstacles in his life to the possibilities.

"I can't see You anymore, God. I can't feel You. I don't even know if You're there." He stopped, feeling a bit silly for saying it out loud. But the questions pressed on his heart. "Are You there? Why don't You help?"

Long seconds passed. He almost thought he could hear a still small voice in the depths of his soul whispering something. Then it was gone, and all Sam could feel was the same heart-rending disappointment he'd felt when God hadn't answered his prayers for Naomi.

"Sam?" Kelly's whispered voice chased away the last fragment of hope. "The girls are waiting for you to kiss them good-night."

"Coming." He tucked the blanket around the sleeping child in the crib then left the room.

"Sam?" Kelly's fingers curled around his sleeve, stopping him. "I'm going to help you with those papers tonight. Abby said we need to have everything in order so there's nothing for anyone to question."

"Yeah, okay." He raked a hand through his hair, wishing he could ignore his duty and escape for a horseback ride. *It's just a few papers,* something inside him reminded. *Possibility.* He inhaled fresh energy. "I'll meet you in the office in ten minutes."

"Okay." She smiled at him, that wide, generous smile that offered friendship and help and encouragement. She was the most beautiful woman he'd ever seen.

Maybe it was time to let go of the past, Sam mused as he walked to the girls' rooms. He'd loved Naomi, but she was gone and there was nothing he could do about it.

Kelly was here, till August anyway, and she was waiting to help him manage whatever obstacles they met. He'd be a fool not to accept her help.

Because Kelly personified possibility.

Chapter Eight

Though Sam tried everything to dissuade her, Kelly insisted on sitting beside him in the tiny room that housed his office.

She whistled at the stacks of papers covering its surface. "You do need help."

"I was always more of a hands-on guy. After Dad got sick, Jake took over most of the bookwork. But now it's a mess," he defended. "Apparently, things lagged a bit after Jacob Samuel's birth, though Jake never said anything. Then he and Marina—" He shrugged, his eyes misty as he stared at the littered desk.

Kelly's heart pinched with compassion. Without even thinking, she reached out and slid her hand into his to share his pain. Sam's fingers curled around hers automatically. He glanced down at their entwined hands then lifted his gaze to hers, his green eyes dark as the forests outside.

"It's okay," she murmured. "We'll handle it, Sam."

"That's your motto, isn't it? We'll handle it." His faint smile gently teased. "I imagine you're great at your job. There must be tons of things that come up, yet I can just see you calmly handling them all with a cheery smile."

"Let's hope that works here," she said as she slid her hand from his to break the rush of sensations his touch brought. She bent over to study the array before her as she listened to his explanation about how the books were organized. "Okay. Got it. So let's see what we have."

Too aware of Sam's scrutiny as she sifted through the papers and organized them in several piles, Kelly kept her head down as she worked and ordered her brain to concentrate instead of reacting to his closeness.

"You're putting this all on a spreadsheet program, so why do you need so many paper copies?" she asked after finding a third series of duplicate medical bills.

"I'm worried I'll miss something," Sam admitted. "It's been years since I trained in this program, and I haven't used it for ages. I'm sure Jake's updated it many times. He—" He stopped, swallowed then shrugged. "I told you I'm the hands-on part of this operation. Paperwork isn't my forte."

"A bonus about my cruise line is their technical side." Sam's blank look told Kelly his ineptitude had nothing to do with ability. It was probably like his fear of cooking; he'd simply never learned how.

"Kelly?"

"Sorry. Daydreaming." She summoned a smile while trying to get back her focus.

"Of traveling." Sam nodded. "I don't blame you."

"Actually, that wasn't it but never mind," she said, unwilling to explain she'd been dreaming about him. "Anyway, the cruise line always has updated computers and on days at sea, staff offers guests classes to learn the latest versions of programs. I've trained on this program. I'll give you a refresher."

Sam grumbled about having to sit when he could be out riding. He grumbled about following her detailed instructions and about his many mistakes. But when he finally caught on, his appreciation warmed her heart.

"This isn't as bad as I thought." He beamed with accomplishment.

"Of course it isn't." Too conscious of the current of attraction running between them, Kelly grabbed a file folder from the pile on the corner of his desk. "Now let's get this one sorted. Medical Bills," she read and flipped it open. She reached for the triplicate invoices she'd seen earlier, but he lifted them out of her hands.

"Uh, I can handle that." Why was Sam acting as if he didn't want her to see them?

"You sure?" Kelly waited for his nod. "Okay. Keep inputting that data while I go check on the kids."

"I didn't hear anything." He leaned toward the baby monitors.

"Neither did I. That's why I'm checking." As Kelly hurried away, she puzzled over the medical invoices she'd glimpsed. The amounts were staggering. The tiny bit of information she'd seen showed the bill had to do with Marina's attempts to have a baby. What was Sam hiding?

Sadie and Emma lay fast asleep in their beds, their cherubic faces precious in the soft glow of the night-light. Kelly straightened their blankets, pressed a kiss to their foreheads and moved on to Jacob Samuel's room. He was awake, kicking his legs and drooling.

"Hey, sweetie. You're supposed to be asleep." A rush of love swept over Kelly. She scooped him into her arms and pressed a kiss against his velvety cheek. What a precious baby he was. She quickly changed him. In the middle of that, she happened to glance up at the picture over the baby's crib. Marina gazed at them with a sweet smile.

"I wish you were here to guide him," Kelly whispered, suddenly overwhelmed by the thought that her sister would never kiss this precious boy again. "It should have been me who died. I wish you were here instead of me."

"Don't say that." Sam stood in the doorway, his face tight with anger. "Don't ever say that, Kelly."

"I'm sorry." She finished sliding on Jacob Samuel's fresh night suit then tucked him back in his crib. "Good night, sweetie." Kelly left the room after one last glance at her sister's face.

"Why did you say that, Kelly?" Sam had closed the door behind her. Now he was studying her, his gaze stern.

"Sometimes I feel like an interloper, like I've done exactly what my mother accuses me of and stepped into my sister's life. It feels wrong. Jacob Samuel is so sweet, and Marina's not here to see and…" She gulped, wishing she could control her tears better. "She should be. I miss her so much. If I could just have said goodbye—"

"Don't go there, Kelly." Sam pulled her into his arms and held her, offering a few moments of quiet refuge. But his embrace did nothing to calm her. In fact, her heart rate soared. "And don't wish yourself dead," he whispered hoarsely. "That wouldn't help anyone, especially me. I've come to value you a lot."

There was such tenderness in Sam's voice, his touch so affectionate, so gentle. She could have stood in his arms much longer, savoring the comfort he offered until she remembered the invoices.

"Sam?" She drew away slowly. "Can I ask you something?"

"I guess." He followed her down the hall and waited until she sat at the desk.

"Are those medical invoices for Marina's treatments to have a baby?" He grimaced then nodded. "Why hide them from me?" She glanced at the columns of figures on the computer and did a quick calculation. "They're marked paid and yet there wasn't enough in either the ranch account or their personal account to cover them."

Sam sat down, but he wouldn't look at her. And suddenly Kelly guessed the truth.

"You paid for my sister's treatments, didn't you?" she whispered, marveling at the debt her family owed him.

Sam was silent for a long time. She thought he wasn't going to answer. Then suddenly he began to speak in a low tone.

"She and Jake were so happy. Marina loved it on the ranch. She pitched in to any task, even cleaning out stalls. Said it made her feel useful." A slanted grin teased his lips for a moment until sadness changed his tone. "She tried to hide her unhappiness at not getting pregnant, but I could see my brother was worried. I pressed him and he finally told me that Marina needed a treatment that was ultraexpensive. It isn't offered here so it wasn't covered by health care. My brother was beside himself trying to figure out a way to make it possible for her to have the baby she wanted. Somebody had to do something for them."

"So you offered to pay for it. But where did you get the money?" Deep in thought, Kelly suddenly noticed a clock on the shelf above them, its parts strewn around. "You're the Fixerator." She saw the truth in his eyes before he ducked his head. "You used the money you earned, your travel savings."

He finally nodded.

"Why would you do that?" she whispered, her heart brimming with affection for this kind, caring man, who was willing to give up his dream so her sister could have hers.

"Because when Jake married her, she became my sister. I wanted her to be happy. I wanted Marina to have her dream," he said quietly.

"At the cost of yours." Kelly turned, wrapped her arms around his neck and drew him close, pressing a kiss against his cheek. "Thank you for giving my sister her dream," she whispered.

"I'm not sure it was me." His arms slid around her waist and held her. She leaned back, curious about his words, and he said, "Marina had the first treatment and nothing happened. I insisted she have another."

"Which you paid for again." *Oh, Sam.*

"Well, yeah. But then the twins came. I think it was their arrival that made her forget about getting pregnant. She was so busy loving them she didn't even realize she was pregnant until the doctor told her." His breathy chuckle disturbed her bangs. "I made fun of her for that."

"But your dream." Still holding him, Kelly focused on his face, on those warm green eyes with golden chips that sparkled whenever he looked at the kids. "What about your dream to travel?"

"Doesn't matter much now, does it?" he asked and let her go, forcing Kelly to release her hold on him. "Even if the twins are taken away, there's still Jacob Samuel to think of. I intend to make sure the Triple D is waiting for him to run if he wants it." His jaw firmed.

"You don't want to travel anymore?" she whispered, unable to believe he'd let go of his lifelong dream so easily.

"Next to the kids, traveling doesn't even compare." Sam cleared his throat and began shuffling papers. "We'd better get back to work."

"Yes." But Kelly's mind was only half on bookkeeping as she watched him enter the figures then file the information. The other half of her brain was busy trying to imagine anyone else she knew doing such a noble, generous thing. Sam was truly a man among men.

Next to Sam's choice to give up his dreams, Kelly felt her decision to leave in August seemed selfish. But what else could she do? This wasn't her home; it wasn't her family. It was just an interlude, a chance to experience everything she'd never have.

And now she realized just how much she would miss.

"That's it, I think." Sam leaned back, surveyed his work and smiled. "I can take this to the accountant tomorrow. Thank you, Kelly."

"I didn't do much." She smiled at him. "Okay, I kept pushing you. But it was for the kids, to make sure everything's in place if and when someone comes to examine things."

"Yeah." Sam fell silent, studying the keyboard. "I realize that and I'm grateful. I'm willing to do anything I can to ensure they don't leave."

"I know. Me, too." She rose. "I'll check on the kids then head to bed."

"Can I ask you something?" The words seemed to spill out of him.

"Sure." Kelly waited.

"About the kids—I mean, how far are you willing to go to ensure they stay?" Sam's voice sounded ragged, edged with frustration, as if he was battling something.

"I don't know what you mean." Was this some kind of test? Kelly frowned.

"I've been thinking about what Abby said. There's this great-aunt now. She seems determined to get custody and, well…" He shifted then rose to pace across the room. "If worse comes to worst, if there is no alternative…"

"Sam." Frustrated by the non-completion of his sentence and by the horrible feeling that something was wrong and she couldn't figure out what, Kelly glared at him. "Just say it," she begged.

"I was wondering if we should get married."

Sam mentally kicked himself. He shouldn't have asked her like that. He should have couched it in better terms, softer, more romantic terms. Women liked that.

Only this wouldn't be a romantic marriage, and Sam

didn't want Kelly to think that was what he was propos-
ing, because he couldn't love her.

"I beg your pardon?" Kelly said it slowly, enunciating
as if she wasn't sure she'd understood. "Did you just—?"

"Ask you to marry me?" He shook his head, saw her
eyes flare wide with surprise and gulped. "No. Well, sort
of." *Get a grip, man!*

Kelly looked at him as if he'd suddenly grown two heads,
neither one containing a brain.

"Actually, what I was asking was if you'd be prepared to
get married if there was no other way to keep the twins."
That was clear enough, wasn't it?

"I'm sorry, Sam." Her brown eyes studied him for a long
time before she ducked her head as if she didn't want him
to see what she was hiding. "I don't think that's a good
enough reason for marriage."

"You don't think keeping the twins here is worth getting
married for?" he demanded, anger swooping in.

"I'm sorry, but I don't." Kelly's voice dropped. "Marriage is a solemn covenant between two people and God. It
shouldn't be undertaken for any reason except that they love
each other and want to spend the rest of their lives together."

Sam couldn't stop his snort of disbelief.

"What does that mean?" Her brows drew together to
give him a dark glare.

"Arranged marriages happened all the time in the Old
Testament," he said and knew from her huff of disgust that
she wasn't impressed by that argument. "People today get
married for all kinds of reasons, not just because they've
fallen in love. Companionship, children, to share expenses."

Sam stopped because Kelly was laughing—at him.

"You want us to get married so we can share expenses?"
she teased.

"I'm not saying we should get married. I'm asking if it

would be a possibility *if* there was no other way to keep the twins," he snapped.

"I'm not prepared to go there, Sam." Kelly hugged her arms around herself as if she was chilled. "I intend to keep praying about it, to keep waiting to hear and see what God will do. I'm not going to invent a solution because I'm afraid to trust His will. I believe God has a plan," she said earnestly. "I want to find out what it is because His way is always best."

She rose and stepped toward the door. Partly because he was frustrated by her pat answer and partly because he just wanted to get the whole mess settled, Sam lashed out.

"Is that the whole truth, Kelly? Or is it that you're afraid to get married, afraid to stick around in one place for more than a few months lest you get tied down and don't get to live the high life anymore?"

Sam knew the moment he said it that he should have kept his lips zipped. Astonishment followed by hurt rolled across her face. Her words, when she finally spoke, oozed pain.

"No, that's not why, Sam." Her voice cracked, but she kept speaking, slowly, carefully, choosing her words with great care.

"Then why?" he asked, hoping she'd explain.

"Because I've learned that forcing things to get my own way ends up causing problems." Kelly paused, her gaze on something in the past.

"Tell me." He didn't think she would until he heard her heavy sigh.

"Four years ago I was ready to toss away everything I believed in, the career I'd worked so hard to achieve, friends I cherished—I was going to give it all up in order to make my dream of being loved come true. I'd planned for everything, certain I could overcome all the barriers that kept us apart. And I was willing to suffer whatever I had to if it got me what I wanted." She stared at him. "That's how badly I wanted to belong, to have a home and someone who cared about me."

"But you had a home. Your parents love you. You belonged." Even as he said it, Sam knew it wasn't true. Something had happened the night of the wedding, something that drove her away and kept her from coming back.

Kelly shed no tears. Her voice was clear and firm, her face stoic as she spoke.

"I didn't belong, Sam." She said it sadly. "But I wanted to so badly that I was willing to leave my friends and live on an isolated island where I knew no one, a place my husband would only visit between sea voyages. I figured that was okay because he'd come home to me. I'd belong to him. He'd love me." She sighed, managed a half smile. "He didn't believe in God but that was okay, too, because I was sure I could win him over. I didn't pray for God's will to be done. I prayed for God to do my will."

Sam waited on tenterhooks, afraid to hear her next words and yet needing so badly to know what had changed for Kelly. "What happened?"

"The day we were to be married I was in an accident. I wasn't badly hurt, but I couldn't get to our meeting place in time. When I did arrive he wasn't there. I waited and waited but he didn't come. I barely made it back to the ship. That night a friend, one of the crew whose warnings I'd disregarded, told me he'd been praying God would stop me. He'd learned that morning that my *fiancé* was married. His wife had arrived unexpectedly to spend the day with him. He already had a *wife*, a *home* and *four children*, whom he rarely saw. This was my dream husband, the one I was giving up everything for."

"I'm so sorry." He couldn't think of anything else to say to wipe away the wounded look in her eyes.

"So am I. Sorry that I didn't trust God and wait for Him to give me the desires of my heart. I came so close to ruining my life because I tried to make things happen my way, in my time." She looked straight at Sam. "You once asked me why God didn't stop pain. Maybe it's because He knows we're too stupid to learn any other way."

Sam didn't know what to say to that.

"Yet even though I didn't wait for God's plan to happen, even though I tried to work everything out myself, God prevented me from making the biggest mistake of my life." Kelly chuckled. "He put me at the scene of an accident where I couldn't escape. That's what saved me."

"So that's why you're determined to wait on God," Sam murmured, more to himself than to her. But Kelly nodded.

"God has a plan for us. We don't have to go searching or trying to make things work, because 'All things work together for those who love God.'" She smiled at him and it was like the sun appearing after a fierce storm. "What we have to do, Sam, is trust Him, wait for His will to be done. You don't have to marry me to keep the twins. If God wants that, He'll find a way to make it happen. If He doesn't, then He's got something better in store. Trust Him."

Easy to say, he thought to himself. Hard to do.

"I'm going to bed," Kelly said between yawns. "Good night."

He let her get as far as the doorway. "Kelly?" She turned, arched a questioning eyebrow. "Thank you. I appreciate you trusting me with your story. There's just one thing I want to add."

"Oh." She looked at him, her big brown eyes wide.

"Wherever you go, wherever you are, know that you will always belong here. From now on I'd like you to consider the Triple D as home. You'll always be welcomed back."

He wasn't prepared for the spill of tears down her cheeks. But her gentle smile spoke volumes.

"Sam Denver, you are the most generous, kindhearted man I've ever known. It's no wonder Marina loved being here with you. I share that feeling." Then with one last look, Kelly turned and left.

Kelly loved him? He stood transfixed by the thought as a tidal wave of pure pleasure rushed through him. Until reason returned.

Love him *as a brother-in-law*. That was what she'd meant.

But that wasn't the way Sam thought of her. Not anymore.

Something had changed inside Sam. Something made him wish for what his brother had found. Peace. Contentment. Happiness.

When he looked through the window of the future, he saw Kelly racing across the grass, chased by the twins and Jacob Samuel. He saw her standing next to him, coffee mug in hand as the twins came downstairs on Christmas morning, eager to see what made their stockings bulge. When cattle stocks declined, as his parents aged, when drought held the land in its grip—through all these times, good and bad, Sam saw Kelly, standing there, buffeted by the wind but strong, dependable.

There for him.

For a long time Sam struggled to make sense of his whirling thoughts. But nothing seemed to compute, so finally he switched off his computer and the desk light, left the room and trudged to his house, to the little log place he'd built for Naomi.

She was a memory now. A blessed memory that he cherished in a private part of his heart. But here, today, the rest of his world seemed filled with Kelly, teasing him for eating the whole pie, hugging him for caring about the kids, placating her mother so she'd stop badgering him.

Kelly had become an integral part of his world, and now he couldn't imagine the future without her.

Chapter Nine

"Happy Mother's Day, Auntie Kelly." Sadie held out a hand-painted picture that had a lopsided bow stuck to one corner.

"Happy Mother's Day," Emma repeated, holding up her own creation to be admired.

"Oh, my goodness. Thank you." Kelly gulped down her surprise and her tears to savor this special moment. "How lovely. You girls did an amazing job. I'm going to hang these on the fridge where everyone can see them." She did so, hugged each of them and listened to their explanations about their artistry as they ate their cereal, thinking how precious it was to be part of this. When she looked up, she found Sam grinning at her. "What's funny?"

"You. You take delight in everything." His hand, wrapped around Jacob Samuel's, clutched a bouquet of flowers, which he held toward her so that the baby couldn't eat them. "These are from him. For you. Because you've mothered him so well."

Kelly took the flowers, sniffed appreciatively then leaned forward to brush a kiss against the baby's cheek. "Thank you, darling."

"Hey, Oscar and I helped him," Sam said with a grin.

"Thank you, Sam. I'll thank Oscar later." She pretended

not to hear his rumble of complaint. She also kept a little distance between them as the memory of his words last night still rang inside her head.

"You always look beautiful, Kelly, but this morning I see dark smudges under your eyes." Sam frowned. "Did you stay up too late last night?"

"Never went to bed." Jacob Samuel was fussing, so she scooped him from Sam's arms, set him in a walker, tied on a bib and handed him a biscuit. "This guy's teething. We walked the floor after you left."

"You should have called me. I could have spelled you off." Sam frowned at her. "It's too much for you to have the parents here for lunch today."

"Not at all." She checked to be sure the salads she'd made yesterday were sitting ready in the fridge and heaved a sigh of relief. She didn't want to give her mother any reason for negative comments. "Since it's so warm, we might want to eat outside at the picnic table. That will mean hauling dishes and food out there. Are you up for manning the grill?"

"Seriously?" He flexed his arm. "I can do that with one hand tied."

"You might have to if your other hand is holding him," she said, meaning Jacob Samuel. Suddenly, she saw the time. "Girls, we have to leave for church. Now."

Both Sadie and Emma appeared, smudges on their cheeks.

"What were you doing?" Kelly grabbed a wet cloth and scrubbed away the mess, though regretfully the marks on their dresses seemed there to stay.

"Making pictures for Gran and Grannybell," Sadie said.

"But you made those yesterday." Regretting the comment when Sadie launched into a long explanation about touch-ups, Kelly held up a hand. "Tell me later, okay? We have to leave now."

Naturally, the service was dedicated to mothers. Pastor Don spoke eloquently of the role mothers played in the lives of their kids, and Kelly realized anew the many things her mother had done to enrich her life. His words also offered perspective on the faith a mother needed to instill in her kids, making Kelly wonder who would do that for the twins and Jacob Samuel.

A deep yearning rose inside, a longing to be able to stay, to share raising the kids with Sam. His question about marriage wouldn't leave her brain. If only it was that easy. If only he could love her.

Of course he hadn't really proposed, only offered it as a last resort, so he wouldn't have to wait and trust God. And yet… She told herself to concentrate on the sermon, to soothe Jacob Samuel's discomfort. But then Sam took him out and there was nothing to stop her brain from dwelling on how perfectly wonderful it would be to stay in Buffalo Gap, on the ranch, with Sam.

Kelly squeezed her eyes closed. She couldn't marry Sam. The weeks she'd spent in Israel, searching for answers about her future, had taught her that her decisions had to be based on God's leading. And while she knew that marriage to Sam would be wonderful, she also knew he couldn't offer her the solid love she'd craved her whole life. Marrying Sam was not God's leading. Perhaps He wanted her to learn to be satisfied with the life He'd given her.

But then why did these soft feelings for Sam keep growing inside her? Life with him on the ranch felt more right than anything had for a very long time, despite tiring nights with a fractious baby and days of keeping the twins entertained. Her life of travel now seemed dull compared to ten minutes showing the kids the first crocus pushing through the earth, celebrating Easter together or marking their heights on the office wall for tangible evidence that they were growing.

Kelly found deep satisfaction in sharing those special moments with Sam. His hearty laugh and constant appreciation were a balm to her lonely heart. Sam never decried her efforts or made her feel excluded. On the contrary, thanks to him the Triple D had become the one place in all these years where she felt comfortable, at home. So much so that she'd secretly persuaded Oscar to give her riding lessons. One summer's day before she left she wanted to see the ranch with Sam via horseback. With Sam, Kelly felt free to be herself, to laugh or cry or simply savor the moments. Now that Marina's videos had filled in her family's past, it had become harder to imagine life anywhere but on the Triple D, with Sam.

But he didn't love her.

Kelly offered a prayer for courage to trust God to parent the kids more perfectly than any human ever could. *Wait upon the Lord.*

"Are you asleep?" Sam nudged her shoulder, jerking her from her inner thoughts. The congregation had risen.

She rose, gave him a droll look, took the edge of the hymn book he held out and sang along with everyone else.

At the end of the service, older children moved through the congregation, passing out carnations to moms. Kelly noticed her own mother, seated next to Mayor Marsha, eagerly reach for the bloom and bury her nose in its petals. Then Arabella lifted her head and looked directly at Kelly, a smile on her lips.

Startled, Kelly smiled back. At least the two of them had progressed far enough to be able to smile at each other. She rode back to the ranch with a song in her heart.

"What can I do to help?" her mother asked the moment she and Neil arrived. "Why, he's teething," she said when Jacob Samuel sobbed. "Hold him a minute longer, Sam, then I'll take him. I know just the thing to help."

Sam blinked and looked at Kelly in surprise. She shrugged

as Arabella pulled an orange from the fridge and peeled it. She took the baby and let his gums rest against the cool, juicy orange. After a moment to adjust to the cold, Jacob Samuel smacked his lips and began heartily sucking. Arabella grinned at them.

"Kelly went through a terrible time teething," she explained. "This was the only thing that gave her relief."

"Thank you, Mother." Kelly leaned over and kissed her cheek. "I'm about at my wit's end trying to make him comfortable."

Arabella blinked. "Oh. Well, I have lots of tips. I'll make some notes for you. Though I don't suppose you'll be here much longer, will you?"

"Awhile yet," Kelly said, tamping down her chagrin. "Come on, Sam. Let's get lunch on the table."

"I've got the fire going. The girls will soon be able to roast their wieners. What else needs to go out?" he asked agreeably, though a frown furrowed his forehead.

Neil and Jock also offered their help, and soon the salads and her mother's favorite cold cuts were ready. Kelly lifted her freshly baked rolls from the oven, proud they'd turned out so light and fluffy. Sam carried the high chair outside, where Arabella set Jacob Samuel in it then insisted she sit beside him. When everyone was seated at the table, Sam spoke.

"Today's a day for mothers. We're very thankful to you, Mom, and to you, Arabella. You gave us life. You taught us how to live it." He held up his glass of juice. "Thank you both."

Plastic glasses clinked against each other, especially the twins', who went round the table. Then, to Kelly's surprise, Sam asked them to sit so *he* could say grace. Amazed that he was actually talking to God, her heart sang as the family shared a meal that was not only delicious but fun, too.

"I love this salad, Kelly." Arabella took another small

helping. "I've never had anything like it. Where did you get the recipe?"

"One of the chefs on the ship used to make it. It's very simple." Marveling that they could have such a calm conversation, she decided to use the opportunity. "I have a gift I made for you, Mom."

"You *made* it?" Arabella accepted the bag and pressed away the tissue paper. She gaped at Kelly. "You quilt?"

"Not like you. I could never manage that," she said quietly. "I make art quilts."

"It's stunning." Her mother held up the picture of her and her husband with Marina in front.

"I copied a picture Marina had. You look good in that shade of blue, and Dad's eyes twinkle against the navy suit. Of course, Marina always looked great." Would using Marina's picture make her efforts acceptable?

"It's beautiful." Her mother delicately traced the lines of stitching with one forefinger. "I've never seen anything so exquisite. Thank you." Then she lifted her head, a frown on her face. "But why aren't you in the picture, Kelly?"

Her mother actually wanted her to be part of the family picture? Kelly grappled with the thought, fully aware that everyone was staring at her, waiting for an answer.

"Oh, uh, you know. I, uh, never think I look like myself. It's easier to do others," she stammered.

"But you're part of our family, Kelly," her father said in a soft voice. "You should be in the picture."

The words burned a path straight to her heart. Kelly gulped and forced herself to speak in a lighter tone.

"Thank you, Daddy. Maybe someday I'll do one of me." She glanced at the twins, now smeared with chocolate icing from the cake Sam had bought to mark Mother's Day. "If I have time," she added with a chuckle.

"I hope you do," her mother murmured, running a finger

over Marina's chin. She lifted her head and studied Kelly. "I really hope so. Thank you."

"You're welcome," she whispered with a full heart, so happy God had worked this softening in her mother.

Sam winked at her, sharing in the moment. Then he presented his mother with a bouquet of her favorite spring flowers and two cookbooks she'd been wanting.

"Not that you need cookbooks," he added. He opened one and flipped to the section on desserts. "I'm hoping you might lend it to me, because ever since this book arrived, I've been salivating over this recipe for pineapple upside-down cake."

"My son the baker," Verna teased. "I'll lend it if you let us sample your cake."

"Deal." He leaned back in his lawn chair with a smug look and promptly toppled backward. Face chagrined, he rose, dusted off his jeans then shared the twins' laughter before turning to the parents. "I wonder if you'd mind babysitting for a while."

"Sam, I—" Kelly stopped when he raised his hand.

"I thought you might show me how far you've come in your riding lessons." His eyes danced with fun at her frown.

"You know?" she demanded.

"Do you honestly think anything goes on around this spread that I don't know about?" he asked with a cocky smile. He glanced at the other adults. "So? Is it doable?"

"Of course." Arabella answered for everyone. "Go and have some fun, Kelly, if you can stay awake. Teething isn't easy on anyone."

Given no choice when the others agreed, Kelly went inside to change. Sam waited at the door for her, but when she was about to pull on her sneakers, he handed her a big box.

"What's this?" She lifted the lid and found a pair of bright red cowboy boots inside. "Red?" she asked, glancing at him.

"It's your favorite color, isn't it?" He chuckled at her blink of surprise. "I told you, I know what's happening on my own place."

"They're beautiful, Sam." Kelly lifted out the boots, admiring the tool work that skipped and danced in a floral pattern up the sides. She pulled one on and found it fit perfectly. She glanced at him questioningly.

"Sheena helped with the size," he told her. "But you can return them if they don't fit right."

"They're perfect." She rose and gazed at her boots with admiration. "Sam, boots are expensive."

"So is finding someone who loves the kids and is willing to clean up their messes, tell them exciting bedtime stories and walk the floor all night." He stared at her, his green eyes dark and intense as they gazed into hers. "Happy Mom's Day, Kelly. And thank you."

He leaned forward to brush his lips against her cheek but at that exact second, Kelly shifted. His lips touched hers. And suddenly he was kissing her as if she was the most special person in his life. And Kelly was kissing him back.

After the initial contact, Sam hesitated, as if he wasn't sure about her response. Stunned by the longing that rose inside, Kelly drew him closer, unwilling to break whatever bond held her in his arms. And Sam responded, his arms gathering her close and holding her with a firm gentleness that reassured her this could end whenever she wanted it to.

But Kelly didn't want it to end. She felt alive, excited, thrilled, by his embrace. She couldn't get enough of his touch, and when his lips finally drew away from hers, she tilted her head so his lips could graze her jawline. She leaned back just enough to let him.

After too short a time, Sam drew away, his eyes shadowed.

"Sadie's coming," he murmured.

Immediately, Kelly let go of him and stepped back. A

thousand sensations tugged at her, confusing her, leaving her wanting more of his touch, more kisses. She turned away from him and slid her jacket off a peg.

"Auntie Kelly, can we make s'mores?" Sadie stood in the doorway, jaw dropping when she noticed Kelly's boots. "Awesome. Where'd you get 'em?"

"Uncle Sam, and you're right. They are awesome." She eased past Sadie and stepped outside, inhaling the fresh air deeply, desperate to put some distance between them. Jacob Samuel's weeping offered the perfect escape. "It was a nice thought, but I'd better stay and look after the baby," she said without looking at Sam. She jumped when his hand curled around her arm. "What are you—"

"He'll be fine. We're going for a ride now but maybe we'll have s'mores after, Sadie." Sam drew Kelly forward. He tossed, "See you," over one shoulder as he led her to the tack barn, chuckling when she drew her arm away from his touch. "It was just a kiss, Kelly. No biggie."

And that was the problem. Sam's kiss *was* a biggie to her, but it clearly meant little to him.

"Oscar did a good job teaching you." Sam forced his gaze off Kelly's trim figure on the horse and onto the land that had been in his family for three generations. "You ride well."

"Thank you." She beamed as if it was the best compliment he could have given her. "Dancer is a great horse, and this is a gorgeous place to ride. I always had this mental picture of me in the saddle, tearing across some exotic beach at a gallop, the wind streaming through my hair."

Sam gulped. He had no trouble creating the image, but was astonished that sweet innocent Kelly would have daydreamed it. Which proved he didn't know enough about her. Given the way she'd kissed him...

"Emma had a bad dream last night." Kelly's words

jerked him from his fantasy of standing on a moonlit beach with Kelly.

"Another one?" He frowned, hating the frustrated feeling that dogged him because he couldn't figure out what was wrong.

"I was pretty thankful that Jacob Samuel had drifted off. It gave me a chance to cuddle her." Kelly's lips pursed, and her brown eyes narrowed when she turned to glance at him. "She's afraid someone is going to come and take her away, Sam."

"You mean, like steal her?" he asked.

"Like this isn't her forever home," she said softly, her gaze moving to stare into the distance. "Those are her exact words, *forever home*." Kelly sighed. "I did my best to reassure her that we love her and this is her home, but I've been thinking about it and—we have to prepare her and Sadie, Sam. Just in case."

"No." His jaw tightened, and he sat rigidly in the saddle.

"We have to at least make them feel that our love for them won't change, even if they live somewhere else," she pleaded. He shook his head. That made her brown eyes darken. "You're sticking your head in the sand, and it's only going to hurt them. We don't have to tell them some great-aunt wants them to live with her, but we have to tell them that no matter where they go or what they do, for the rest of their lives we'll care about them and always be here for them."

"But you won't be," he snapped and wished he hadn't when she winced, her expression pain filled. "I'm sorry. That didn't come out right," he apologized then tried again. "I meant I don't want to lie to them, but more than that, I don't want them to worry about leaving. They're kids. They should be running and playing, enjoying life. Not cringing in the dark, waiting for someone to take them away from everything they know."

"I know, but—" Kelly reined in her horse and sat staring at him with the saddest look he'd ever seen. "I've prayed so hard," she whispered helplessly.

"I guess sometimes praying isn't enough," he mumbled, feeling as helpless as she did. Seeing they were beside the river, Sam dismounted, walked over to Kelly and held out a hand. "Let's talk here," he said quietly.

He helped her slide off her horse then led her to a boulder he'd sat on at various times throughout his life. When she was seated, he sank down beside her, enjoying the rub of her shoulder against his. This was his thinking place. Maybe together they could find the answers that had eluded them.

"What do we do, Kel? We haven't heard any more from this woman lately. Maybe she's no longer interested in the twins."

Kelly remained silent. Sam sighed and nodded.

"I don't think that's true, either." He threw his Stetson on the grass and lay back against the rock, letting the sun chase away the chill caused by thoughts of losing the twins. "So?"

"I don't have any answers, Sam." A tinge of hopelessness in her voice bugged him. "I don't know where God's leading. The only thing I know to do is to prepare the twins by making sure they know that wherever they go, they'll always be loved."

"Okay, maybe." He chewed a stem of grass, trying to come up with a plan. Then he remembered their picnic lunch. "Your mother seemed to love her picture. She even wanted you in it. I think she's realizing how much she's missed having you in her life."

"It could be." Kelly sounded cautious.

"You don't believe she liked it?" Her attitude confused him.

"I guess, but I'm afraid to trust. I've gone so long believing one thing. It's hard to do an about-face and believe she actually wants me in her life." Kelly closed her eyes and tipped her head back so the sun lit her face.

"What actually happened to make you leave that night, Kelly?" Maybe now, here, alone in this glade, he'd finally understand why she'd left and never come back.

"You don't want to hear my sad past, Sam," she whispered.

He touched her cheek with his knuckles. "Actually, I would."

He watched as she sat up straight, pushed her shoulders back and let out a huge sigh. Then she looked at him, her brown eyes steady, determined.

"She wanted, no, insisted, I go back to Bible college," Kelly said, the words stark. "She said that if I didn't, she and Dad would cut me off. That I'd have to move out."

"Why?" Somehow in all the things Sam had imagined, this had never come up.

"I'd been a little wild when I came back after a summer mission trip and found out your brother was marrying my sister." She hung her head in shame. "I stayed out late, went on drinking sprees, found an unsavory crowd that went against pretty much everything I believe in."

"Because you were hurting about Jake. Because you loved him." He nodded.

"Funny how you understand." Kelly's smile brimmed with sadness. "Mom didn't. She thought I was doing it to spite her. I wasn't. I just couldn't come to terms with the death of my girlish fantasy of love."

"So you acted out before the wedding. Okay. But why take off after the wedding, after that heart-to-heart we shared?" Sam knew from the silence that followed that the answer wasn't easy for her.

"That night, when we arrived home after the wedding, she had guests over." The whisper-soft words brimmed with pain. "Some of my friends showed up a bit later, and I went out drinking with them. I have no excuse except I couldn't take knowing Marina had everything I ever wanted. I came home drunk. I'd never done that before, but I hurt so much. I thought if I drank enough, it would blot out losing Jake."

"I wish you'd called me," he said.

"I wish I had, too." She smiled grimly. "I was half out of it when Mom lit into me. She said I was an embarrassment to the family, always had been." A brokenness in her voice slammed Sam in the gut. "There was a lot of condemnation about how I was a big disappointment. What was there about me to make her proud? I'd never been the stellar student Marina was. I never won a scholarship or shone at public speaking. She had to push me into summer missions, and even there I was only average. I was a year out of school, fresh out of Bible college and I still had no plan for my life, no future goals like her friends' kids. She said she didn't want a daughter she was ashamed of."

Sam sucked in his breath through his teeth, furious at the hurtful words. Shame filled Kelly's face.

"I guess I deserved it. I was an idiot, living on the edge. But to hear her say that…" Her voice broke. She paused, inhaled and knotted her fingers. "It hurt so badly, but I could have taken it. Until she said I'd never find a husband like Marina had because what man would want someone like me, someone who never amounted to anything. She—" Kelly gulped. "She said she was beginning to wish I'd never been born."

Her misery reached right into Sam's heart and sent a powerful rush of affection through him. After nine-plus years, this wonderful woman still felt the sting of those hurtful words. He had to help her.

"Aw, Kel." Sam cupped her face in his palms and pressed a kiss against her lips. "She didn't mean it. She was trying to snap you out of your self-destruction."

"By saying she wished I'd never been born?" Kelly choked back a sob.

"Who can fathom what goes on in your mother's head?" he teased, waiting for the dimple that signaled her smile to peek out. "From what I know of her, I assume she was mixed up at losing her daughter to marriage, probably afraid you'd go, too. Maybe she had to give up her plans for Marina but thought you'd take them on."

"Take Marina's place, you mean?" Kelly looked dubious.

"Perhaps." He brushed the tear from her cheek, handed her a tissue from his pocket. "Does it matter? It's over and done. The past is gone. The 'why' isn't important."

"To me it is," she whispered.

"It shouldn't be. Take it from an expert," he said with a wry smile. "Digging up the past and concentrating on the what-ifs only makes you miserable."

Kelly said nothing, simply watched him with her melting brown eyes.

Sam leaned back on his hands to keep himself from touching her. This woman was like a sweet treat that he couldn't get enough of. Better to keep his distance than to start imagining there could be something between them.

"I've spent aeons of wasted time thinking about Naomi and speculating on what our future might have been," he admitted.

"You don't anymore?" she asked quietly.

"I'm trying not to. Because of you." He smiled when a frown furrowed the smooth skin of her brow. "I'm not ready to turn things completely over to God. I still don't understand His ways."

"Maybe you never will," she murmured.

"But I have learned that 'kicking against the pricks,' as the apostle Paul called it, is painful and pointless. I'm trying to reconcile myself. Naomi's gone. I've given up the dreams we shared. I wouldn't wish her back to go through that pain anyway."

"That's a big step." Kelly's gentle smile made his heart bump a little faster.

"I guess." He struggled to hang on to his composure. "Only, I can't let go of the twins," he admitted, hearing the raggedness in his own voice. "How can it be better for them to leave than it is to stay here where it's home? How can some aunt, even with all her money, be a better parent for them than me? That's what bugs me about God. Why?"

"I don't know what to tell you, Sam." Kelly peered into the distance. "The only thing I know is a verse from Jeremiah that I hang on to in tough times. 'I know the plans I have for you. Plans to prosper you and not to harm you, plans to give you hope and a future.' That's God's promise. His plan is good."

"I wish that was enough for me," he said sadly. "But I can't get rid of this hole in my gut that tells me that I'm going to lose and the twins are going to leave. I'm going to fail my brother, Kelly." He pretended he didn't hear when Kelly promised to keep praying.

They sat together in the silence of the afternoon with only the croak of creek-side bullfrogs. Restless, Sam checked his watch.

"Yes, I suppose we'd better head back," Kelly said with a sigh when she saw him double-check the time.

"Before we go, can you answer just one more of my questions?" Sam waited. He wasn't sure why he needed to know so badly. All he knew was that it mattered. "Why didn't you come back, Kelly? It's been well over nine years, and you still stayed away."

"Because my mother asked me not to." She nodded at his surprise. "It's true. About four years ago I planned to come home. I arranged everything ahead of time to be sure I'd have lots of time to spend with them. When everything

was approved, I let Mom know. She asked me to stay away."
Kelly blinked furiously, and he knew it was a struggle to say
the words. "She said it was better if I didn't come back and
cause trouble. I assured her that I had no intention of causing
any problems, but she was insistent. She didn't want me."

"So you took off for Timbuktu." A deep, burning anger
gripped Sam. She'd missed so much. Why had Arabella—

"Actually, Kathmandu," Kelly corrected with a grin.
She shrugged. "After that, well, I figured it was better if I
stayed away permanently."

"It wasn't better." He rose, held out a hand and drew her
upward. "I'm going to ask your mother why she did that."

"No, Sam." Kelly put a hand on his arm, her voice plead-
ing. "Let it go. Please? As you've just reminded me, the past
is finished. What's the point of dredging it all up again?"
She glanced down at her hand, slowly lifted it away from
him. "We're building a new relationship. I want to work
on that."

He liked her touch. He enjoyed kissing her. He couldn't
stop thinking about those tender times when he'd held her
and marveled at how right she felt in his arms.

That was why he had to ask.

"And us, Kelly? What are we building?"

She stared at him for a fleeting second then ducked her
head down. A moment later she lifted it and looked straight
at him. "Friendship, Sam. A really special friendship."

Then she climbed on her horse and nudged the mare into
a slow canter toward home.

After a moment Sam followed, one thought circling his
brain.

He wanted more than friendship with Kelly Krause.

Chapter Ten

❧

"I'm sorry, Mom. I'd love nothing more than to come and chat with Dad, but Emma isn't feeling well today. I don't think I should expose either of you to her germs." Kelly steeled herself for the arguments she knew would follow.

Living in a different house hadn't diminished her mother's demands one iota. She still called several times a day, usually at the most inopportune moments, waking Jacob Samuel and making demands Kelly often couldn't fulfill. It seemed as if her mother was trying to exact a sort of twisted punishment for all the years Kelly had been unreachable.

"Hilda's sick, too. What about Sam? Can't he stay with the kids?" Arabella insisted.

"I'm sorry, but he can't." Kelly shot a sideways glance at the object of the conversation, who was sitting at the kitchen table, sharing a pink-iced cupcake with Sadie. She'd drawn Sam into her problems often enough. Besides, she was supposed to be here to help him, not add to his work-load. "Sam's got work to do."

"With those blasted cows, I suppose." A cluck of teeth transmitted over the phone. "Sam always puts the animals first."

"Mother, that's not true." Kelly wished her mother wasn't

so negative about this man, who'd only brought comfort and joy to her life.

"You don't want to admit it, Kelly." Arabella's voice hardened. "But if you intend to take Marina's place, to live her life, you'd better learn the truth about the most important thing in Sam's life. That's his cows."

"That isn't true, Mother," Kelly said, thinking of the money Sam had willingly handed over to help Marina. "Anyway, Sam and I are just friends." Her face burned with shame at her mother's insinuation. "I could never take Marina's place, even if I wanted to. Which I don't."

"You two together in *her* house—it isn't right." Her mother heaved a sigh. "I don't have time for this. I can't miss this afternoon's quilt meeting, Kelly. My friend Mayor Marsha insisted I present my pattern on the double wedding ring quilt to the group today. She feels it's the perfect way for our club to win over Calgary's."

Our club?

"I'm sure everyone will enjoy learning about it." Kelly ignored Sam's grin as she resorted to praise. "With your knowledge and skill, they're lucky to have you."

"So you'll come and stay with your father?" Arabella wheedled.

"I can't, Mom. I'm sorry. Maybe you could ask your friend Marsha?" Kelly remained adamant despite her mother's demands, criticisms and outright anger. When the phone slammed down in her ear, she carefully hung up.

"I *could* watch the kids," Sam offered. "An afternoon off from branding won't make a difference."

"Thanks, but I don't want her to think we'll come running every time she demands it." Kelly sat down, gratefully accepting the coffee he'd creamed exactly the way she liked. "I thought I'd phone Abby and see if she has any news."

"You're expecting some?" He raised an eyebrow.

"I'd like to know before tomorrow." Kelly tilted her head slightly sideways to indicate Sadie, who was listening to them with great interest.

"You better not eat any more of these, Uncle Sam, because the rest are for our birthday party tomorrow," the little girl said, proving Kelly's point that it was hard to get anything past her.

"I think we'll have plenty of cupcakes, honey," Kelly agreed, having just finished icing four dozen. "Are you sure you want cupcakes and not a birthday cake?"

"Me an' Emma like cupcakes better," Sadie assured her as she added more sprinkles to the tops.

Still a bit uncertain, Kelly glanced at Sam. "You think they're okay?" she asked.

"They're perfect. Stop worrying. Have I mentioned that I like the way you approach everything as if we're a team?" Sam grinned at her then dabbed a bit of pink icing on Sadie's cheek. The little girl giggled, scrubbed it off then reminded Kelly of her promise to be allowed to watch her favorite Cinderella video.

After settling her on the sofa and starting the program, Kelly returned to the kitchen. The remnants of another cupcake lay on the table, and Sam was wearing his own array of pink icing on the tip of his chin. She grabbed a napkin and held it out.

When he frowned at her, she leaned forward and wiped the icing just as he turned his head. His lips grazed her wrist, sending a stream of sensations up her arm. Overwhelmed by her reaction to him, she jerked back. Sam blinked at her but said nothing.

"As if we're a team?" She sank into a chair opposite him. She had to sit because her knees had turned to a wobbly jelly. "Aren't we a team?"

"Of course." His lazy grin did wonderful things to his handsome face. "You're a good sport, Kelly."

"Uh, thank you." Why did Sam's presence have this odd effect on her? "Emma and Jacob Samuel are sleeping, and I have a few minutes while Sadie's watching her video. Do you have a minute to go over the to-do list for the party tomorrow?"

"Shouldn't you be getting supper ready?" he asked, tongue in cheek.

"Why? It's your night to make supper." She pointed to the menu on Marina's kitchen blackboard then leaned forward. "Erasing it won't change anything, Sam. You're supposed to be learning a varied menu to prepare meals for the kids for when I won't be here," she chided.

"But pot roast?" he protested. "That's tough. Maybe I could hire a cook."

"You don't need one. Pot roast isn't difficult," she promised. "I'll show you then we'll talk about the party."

They worked together side by side, bumping shoulders, brushing each other's hands. But eventually the roast was seasoned and in the slow cooker.

"So later you'll put in potatoes and carrots and they all cook together?" His grin flashed when she nodded. "That makes cleanup a breeze."

"Which will be handy for you when I'm not here to mop up your messes," she teased. "And if you're delayed a little or away for the afternoon, you can still have a hearty, healthy dinner when you get home." He stared at her, and Kelly frowned. "What's wrong?"

"I don't like to think of you not being here," he explained. "You belong on the ranch, with the kids." His voice dropped as he set the cover in place. "Won't you rethink staying?"

"I can't, Sam. I wish I could, but this isn't where I belong." How she hated saying that. Because here, with the kids, on the ranch, Kelly felt totally at home. Yet no matter how she felt, this was not where God wanted her, not permanently. She sighed then picked up the pad with her party plans. "Fishing pond ready? I hope you don't intend to take them to the river," she said mockingly.

"Ha-ha." He made a face. "I borrowed a kid's swimming pool, which Oscar will fill tomorrow morning."

"So no drowning incidents. Imagine that. Possibilities." She smirked when Sam sniffed his disgust. "A campfire? Wiener sticks? Tables and chairs for the kids to sit?"

"Check, check and check. The bubble toys are hidden in the work shed with the kites, as requested. The items for the treasure hunt have been secreted, as directed, including the gold chest, which, I might add, took me forever to make."

"But it will be so worth it," Kelly promised. "The twins are going to have a blast."

"Yes, but you're forgetting the most important thing." Sam leaned in so close their noses almost touched. "Their gifts," he prodded.

"I sewed them each a new summer outfit," she said. It was clear from the twinkle in Sam's eyes that he'd planned something else. "What did you get?"

"Bikes. With training wheels. Both pink because it's their favorite color. Both with streamers and those things that tick when the wheels turn." He grinned, obviously proud of himself. "I thought we could put them outside early tomorrow morning and then think up an excuse so the kids could find them."

"Good idea. And I have enough food to feed an army. I think we're ready." She leaned back in her chair, almost able to let go of the worry that something would spoil the twins' special day.

"We're going to be dead tomorrow evening," he told her with a grin.

"But it will be so worth it." A smug sense of satisfaction rippled through her when she happened to glance through to the living room and caught sight of her sister's smiling face. "They'd be proud of us," she told Sam.

"I hope so." He rose, moved behind her chair and wound his arms around her neck in a hug, pressing his cheek to hers. "They'd be very proud of you. You're amazing, Kelly. There's no one I'd rather have by my side than you."

Though she had no recollection of it, Kelly thought she must have said thank you. Sam must have let go of her and gone back to his branding. Nothing had really changed.

And yet, in those few moments everything changed for Kelly.

Because she was falling in love with Sam Denver.

She couldn't! She had to concentrate on doing what she was here for, had to remember her lesson that romance and everything that went with it was not part of God's plan for her. If it was, wouldn't she know? She'd be certain if it was God's will for her, right?

But this—this affection couldn't be love. Deep friendship, maybe. A solid, firm friendship that had withstood many trials. Of course she cared about Sam. She cared about the twins and Jacob Samuel, too. So maybe it was a love of sorts.

But not the kind of love that couples shared.

That kind of love wasn't for her.

Kelly told herself to focus on tomorrow, on making certain the twins had the most memorable party ever and forget everything but doing her best to be certain this family stayed together.

Because in three months she'd have to leave and return to the path God wanted her to follow, no matter what her heart thought it wanted.

Sam's pride in the Triple D ballooned as kids raced across the lawns to find the treasure box.

"They're going to sleep tonight," his friend Cade chuckled.

"You couldn't have asked for a better day," his wife, Abby, remarked. "Perfect for treasure hunts and fishing and bubbles. You're blessed."

He was blessed? Him? The thought silenced Sam when his gaze landed on Kelly.

"We found it! We found it," Sadie yelled at the top of her voice. She swaggered a little as she lugged the box he'd made and spray painted metallic gold. "But we need a key," she huffed, plopping it at his feet. "How do we get a key, Uncle Sam?"

"Well, mateys, ye pirates will just have to figure it out." He grinned when Kelly rolled her eyes at his attempted pirate accent.

"You just had to complicate it, didn't you?" she said in a droll voice.

"I have good ideas, too, you know." He only half noted her gurgle of laughter because his attention strayed to the dust trail of a vehicle headed his way. "Wonder who that is?"

"I thought everyone who was coming was already here, but maybe someone's late." Kelly's hand slipped into his when a huge black SUV turned into the drive. "I don't know them, Sam," she whispered, her voice tense. "Do you?"

"No." Keeping his voice low wasn't difficult since Sadie and Emma had opened the box and were tossing the gold chocolate coins to their screaming friends. "I'll go check."

Trepidation filled him as he disentangled his hand and walked forward. The door of the vehicle opened as he arrived. A tall, slim woman with gray hair stepped out, followed by an equally tall, equally slim man. The woman held out her hand.

"You must be Sam," she said in a well-modulated voice. "I'm Eunice Edwards. This is my husband, Tom."

A stone dropped into his stomach, heavy and ice cold.

"Yes, I'm Sam. How can I help you?" he asked while inside his heart demanded of God, *Why*?

"We're here for the twins' birthdays," she said. "I phoned this morning to tell you but no one answered, and I couldn't leave a message."

"I guess we forgot to turn on the machine," Sam said automatically. Why couldn't he get a grip on this, make the world come right again?

"Would you prefer we come back later?" Mrs. Edwards asked in a low tone. "We don't want to cause a fuss."

Then leave, his brain screamed. *Go home and don't ever come back.*

"You're welcome to stay, but there can be no discussion about your plans to adopt the twins." He stared at her to ensure she realized he was completely serious. "This is their day in their home, and they're happy. I want them to stay that way, not be lambasted with the worry that someone is going to take them from everything they know and love."

"I understand, Sam. We know this must be a difficult time for you." She nodded, generous, graceful and courteous.

Everything he didn't want her to be. He wanted a villain, a wicked stepmother-type whom he could hate and vilify.

"Sam? Will you introduce us?" Kelly stood by his side, close, as if she was afraid.

"Certainly." He slung an arm around her shoulders, trying to reassure her. "Meet Mr. and Mrs. Edwards, the twins' aunt and uncle, though we won't mention that to anyone here. Not now," he said with a warning look at the couple. "This is Kelly Krause, their aunt, their mother's sister." He put a little emphasis on that last part, to reinforce their claim.

Mrs. Edwards simply smiled and shook hands. "It's very good to meet you, Kelly. May we join the party?"

"Sure," Kelly said swiftly, too swiftly. She glanced from her worn jeans to Sam's and then to the couple's more formal attire. "It's a picnic," she said quietly.

"And we're not dressed for it. Oh, well." Eunice slid out of her jacket and put it in the backseat of the car. She rolled up her sleeves, kicked off her heels and wiggled her bare toes in the grass. Her husband followed suit, except for the shoes. "We'll manage," she said with a smile.

"I'll introduce you to our friends." Sam led them toward Abby and performed the introductions. He saw her eyes flare at the names before she glanced his way. He gave a quick nod and kept moving around the group until all the adults had greeted the interlopers. "Help yourself to a drink, coffee, tea or juice," he said. "Lunch will be in a while. The kids will be having a wiener roast."

"How fun," Eunice Edwards said with a smile. "I see it's bubble time. I haven't done that in years. Do you mind if I join in?"

"You'll have to ask Kelly. She planned the games." He watched Mrs. Edwards walk toward Kelly then turned away, irritation making his jaw tighten.

"I can't believe they came here today," Abby murmured darkly. "I'm going to have a word with someone about this," she promised, hurrying away, phone in hand.

With a sinking heart, Sam observed Sadie's awareness of Mrs. Edwards and her nudge of Emma, whose gaze also tracked the woman. In that moment his goal became crystal clear. Allow nothing to interfere with the joy of this birthday party. He hurried toward Kelly.

"Let's keep the games going as if she wasn't here," he said in a whisper meant for her ears alone. Kelly nodded. "Are we flying the kites now?"

"If you can handle those with Cade while I bring out the cupcakes. It's just about time to feed everyone." She smiled at him and squeezed his arm as if to reassure him that everything was okay. Which didn't work.

"Oh, that reminds me," Mrs. Edwards said from behind

them. "We brought along a birthday cake and a few gifts. We didn't want to show up empty-handed."

You couldn't fault her for manners, Sam thought. There was no trace of guile or trickery in her wide-eyed gaze, no sign from her voice that she was being anything other than honest.

Yet he said, "Let's wait on gifts until after the food." Mrs. Edwards's easy agreement did not reassure him, but there was no time to dwell on it. Twelve little kids wanted to fly kites, so Sam got to work.

But inside he kept asking God, *Why? Why now, why today? Why at all?*

And though he searched for and found Kelly's reassuring smile, a balm to his troubled soul, Sam did not find an answer to his question. Nor, once lunch was underway, could he accept her whispered "Trust God."

Too much was at stake.

"Now that's what I call a birthday cake. Nothing homemade about it."

Kelly tried to ignore her mother's whispered comment as Mr. Edwards set a beautifully decorated fairy princess cake beside her crudely decorated cupcakes. She realized that she'd forgotten the candles inside, but by the time she returned with them, Mrs. Edwards had already lit the candles on the fairy cake and everyone was singing "Happy Birthday" while Sam snapped pictures of the twins and their friends.

Kelly stuffed down her chagrin when a wide-eyed Sadie commented to Emma about the pretty cake the "lady" had brought. If they liked cakes so much why had they chosen cupcakes? She chided herself for being petty then forced a smile as Sam snapped a picture of her with the twins.

Once everyone had finished their cake and ice cream, Kelly assembled the kids in a circle on the grass so the twins could open their gifts. She couldn't suppress her pride when they dutifully thanked each giver. She quietly slipped her own gift out of the stack and into the bottom of a closet after the girls opened Eunice Edwards's gifts. No way did Kelly want someone to compare her handmade outfits with the Edwards's designer shirts and jeans as they'd compared her cupcakes and their fancy cake. Okay, so she was insecure—she was also afraid.

As the kids raced off to swat the piñata Sam had hung from the old oak tree, Kelly and Abby cleared the tables with the other moms.

"Isn't it amazing?" one mom said to another. "That fancy cake and all those expensive clothes. Marina never mentioned well-to-do relatives."

"Ignore them, Kelly," Abby whispered. "You did a wonderful job."

"Thanks, but even my own mother is impressed." She inclined her head to where Arabella was raving about the Edwards's stylish car.

"I'll fix that." Abby hurried toward Verna, and a few moments later that woman escorted Arabella into the kitchen on the pretext of amusing a cranky Jacob Samuel. "A reprieve." Abby grinned when she returned.

"You're a good friend." Kelly hugged her.

Finally, the Edwardses said goodbye, promising the twins they'd see them again soon.

"Perhaps you girls could come for a visit," Eunice offered, glancing at Sam from her hunkered-down position face-to-face with Sadie. "We could go to the zoo. There are a lot of fun things to do where we live."

Kelly heard the words with dismay, her worries building when she glanced at Emma. The little girl's face paled as she reached out to grasp Sadie's hand and moved to stand behind her.

"I think we'll talk about that another time." She held

Mrs. Edwards's gaze with an unflinching look until that woman finally nodded. "Now say goodbye, girls, then we need to thank your other guests."

Sadie dutifully thanked them for their gifts, particularly the computer tablet they'd received. Emma whispered "thank you," still cowering behind Sadie.

"It was nice to meet you." Kelly wrapped an arm around Emma's shoulder. "Please excuse us now. We have to hand out the treat bags."

"Of course. I hope we'll see you again," Mrs. Edwards said. "I understand you're leaving in August."

The words made Kelly furious, but her first concern was for the twins. She ignored the couple to usher the girls away.

"What did she mean, Auntie Kelly?" Sadie demanded. "Where are you going?"

"I'm not going anywhere for a long time," Kelly told her, trying to infuse reassurance into her words. Seeing Sadie's dissatisfaction and Emma's growing worry, she knelt on the ground and pulled the twins into a tight embrace while mentally whispering a prayer for the right words. "Look, you two. You know I love you, right?"

Sadie nodded first, then Emma, more slowly.

"So I would never want to hurt you." Loving the way they leaned into her, she kissed each brow. "But the man I work for only gave me so many holidays, and then I will have to go back to work. Uncle Sam's work is here but mine is on a ship, far away."

"Like the princess story," Emma whispered.

"Kind of." A group of boisterous kids were headed their way. "I'll tell you more about it later, after the party's over and your friends have gone home. Okay?"

They both nodded, but serious questions lingered in their blue eyes. Kelly rose, watching the twins leave with their friends. Emma paused and glanced over her shoulder, as if to ensure that Kelly was still there. That action brought tears to Kelly's eyes.

"I thought you were handing out treat bags?" Sam murmured from behind her.

"They are. See?" She dashed away a tear then pointed to where Sadie was distributing the bags Kelly had hidden under the table. Emma stood apart, alone, her gaze fixed on Kelly and Sam. Kelly's heart bumped for the child's sadness. Somehow Emma knew the truth; she was convinced of that.

Kelly let out her pent-up frustration on a sigh. "Why did the woman have to say that about me going?"

"Mrs. Edwards apologized. She said they thought the twins knew everything, including their intention to adopt." Sam's lips pressed tightly together, but his voice remained calm. "Thanks for not letting your irritation show. I feel the same, but it wouldn't have done our case any good to show it."

"They must have seen the girls' birthdates on the adoption forms they filled out. But why did they come here?" she demanded.

"To make it clear that they have the financial clout to care for the kids far better than we can?" He shrugged. "Abby's trying to get some kind of restraint so they can't just show up here again, but I doubt it will work."

Kelly didn't argue because she had the same doubts. "What are we going to do, Sam?"

"Keep on loving them, caring for them." He draped an arm around her shoulder and hugged her to his side. "What else can we do?"

"Pray," she murmured, leaning in to his warmth, hoping it would take away the chill she felt. Every nerve in her body was aware of this man. She longed to throw herself into Sam's arms and wallow in his care. But he didn't love her.

"Praying hasn't done us much good," he said darkly as he lifted away his arm. "But if it makes you feel better, go ahead. I don't think things could get any worse." He clasped her forearms so that she had to face him. "Kelly, are you sure you can't marry me?"

Hope ballooned inside her. Maybe he did feel something…

"For the twins?" he added.

"Sam, I don't want them to leave any more than you do." It hurt so much to say that, to reject the one thing she wanted to do most—stay with him, marry him, live here with the twins. "But I don't believe marrying you is the answer."

"Then what is?" he demanded, his hands falling away.

"I don't know." Kelly peered into his beloved face. If only… "But I believe God has a reason for this," she said quietly. "We just have to trust Him."

She tried to instill strength into her voice, but inside, her faith was shrinking. She couldn't stay here, marry Sam. Okay, she'd accept that. Somehow. But surely God didn't want the twins to leave their home?

As Kelly stood by Sam's side to thank parents and children for coming to the twins' birthday, she stored the memory of being with him, shoulder to shoulder, sharing every precious moment of this day.

She would need his strength and support for their upcoming discussion with the twins.

Chapter Eleven

"So that's why Mr. and Mrs. Edwards came," Sam summarized after he'd explained the twins' relationship to the couple that evening. "They're your family and they want to get to know you."

Hoping he'd said all the right things, he glanced at Kelly and found her attention riveted on Emma. The little girl had said nothing during the past hour that he and Kelly had spent with them in the family room. She'd kept one hand tightly clasped around Sadie's, her blue eyes moving from person to person as she listened, her worry obvious.

"But they asked us to visit them. I don't want to," Sadie said, her voice whiny. "Do we have to?"

Sam looked to Kelly for help. It seemed that lately he was always doing that. When Kelly rose and left his side, it felt as if he was losing his right arm. He depended on her so much. She sat between the twins and wrapped one arm around each girl, snuggling them close. To his relief, some of Emma's sadness seemed to melt when she dredged up a smile for her aunt.

"Listen, my dear girls. Uncle Sam and I love you very much. We want you to be happy because we want the very best for you. Getting to know your family is a good thing.

We don't want you to be afraid," she said with a wide smile and repeated, "Family is good."

Where did she get this assurance? Sam wondered. She, who'd found family such a trial? At the moment Kelly seemed perfectly fine with the Edwards's visit, and yet he knew that wasn't true. Had she attained this newfound strength because of the prayers she said earlier when he'd seen her kneeling by her bed? Did she really believe God was going to somehow come through for them?

"We want our family around us," she continued, her voice filled with love as her fingers brushed the flaxen curls. "They love us and help us be strong. When we're with family, we're home."

"This is my home," Sadie said stoutly, her lips set. "I don't know that lady and man."

Sam held his breath, wondering how Kelly would answer.

"Listen, sweetie." Kelly lifted the little girl onto her lap. "When you and Emma first came to the ranch, you didn't know Mommy and Daddy, either, did you?"

Sadie thought about it.

"No," Emma whispered.

Sam couldn't stop himself. He needed to be part of this, so he rose, walked across the room and swung Emma into his arms before settling beside Kelly. This was his family, he thought with a fierceness that surprised him.

Kelly blinked at his closeness, but when she smiled Sam's worries diminished and suddenly he was certain the twins' questions weren't too hard. The problems ahead seemed a little less insurmountable with Kelly beside him. They could handle it.

"You had never met Mommy and Daddy before, but they became your family, didn't they?" Kelly waited for the twins' nods of agreement. "How did that happen?"

"I dunno." Sadie stared at her blankly.

"How about you, Em?" he asked the child in his arms. "Do you know how they got to be your mom and dad?"

Emma shook her head. Her tiny hand slid into his, seeking, he was certain, reassurance.

"Tell us how it happened, Auntie Kelly." Sam was completely willing to go along with her on this because he trusted her. He was comfortable with leaving Kelly to explain because she had a knack for making things all right.

What would he do when she left?

"It happened because God gave you love to make you a family. Just like He made us a family." Kelly waved her hand around in a circle to include the four of them. For an instant her brown gaze clung to his, and Sam couldn't have looked away, even if he'd wanted to.

"An' Jacob Samuel?" Sadie asked.

"Of course Jacob Samuel is part of our family." Kelly hugged her. "See, God takes Sadie and Emma and Jacob Samuel and Kelly and Sam and Gran and Grandpa and Grannybell and Grandpa Neil, and he puts them all together into a family who loves each other and takes care of each other. And that's what makes a family. Right, Sam?"

Kelly lifted her head and stared directly at him as if she was trying to tell him something important. Only he couldn't figure out what it was. And he wanted to. He wanted to know what gave her face that soft glow, lent her eyes that sheen and softened her manner to that inviting look that drew him to her.

"So you mean God wants that lady and man to be our fam'ly?" Sadie asked before Sam could respond to the question.

"I think maybe He does," Kelly said thoughtfully. "And I think they want to be part of your family, too. I think they're lonely."

"'Cause they don't gots no little girls?" Emma whispered then nodded. "They gave us lots of presents so we'd like them."

"Mouths of babes." Sam studied his niece in amazement. Such a little bit of a thing, yet Emma saw to the heart of the matter.

"They were really nice presents." Sadie thought for a moment then asked in a half-fearful voice, "Is that why you think we should go visit them, Auntie Kelly?"

"Because of gifts?" Kelly shook her head. "No. That's not a good reason. You visit someone because you want to see them, because you care about them."

Sam frowned at her but Kelly ignored him.

"Maybe if they ask again, we'll talk about it then." Her bright smile chased away the shadows he'd seen in her eyes. "But that isn't something you have to worry about."

"How come?" Emma asked, her blue eyes narrowing.

"Because if you do go to see the Edwardses, you'll be taking part of your family with you." Kelly chuckled when Emma twisted to peer at Sam. "No, not Uncle Sam. I'm sure he'd love to go, but he has to stay on the ranch. I meant God. He goes with us wherever we go, so He'd be right there on the visit with you."

"Oh." Sadie looked at Emma. They considered what she'd said for a few minutes before Emma nodded.

"Can we have the princess story now, Auntie Kelly?" Emma asked in a voice significantly louder than it had been before.

Shocked by this change, Sam glanced at Kelly, who was smiling at him with a knowing glint in her eyes. She gave a little nod before she turned to the twins.

"You're not too tired for a story after such a busy day?" Their aunt laughed when two blond heads shook an emphatic denial. "Okay, then. Well, today was the princess's birthday."

"Same as ours!" Sadie cheered. She and Emma high-fived each other.

"Yes, but you see," Kelly began in a serious voice, "the princess's boat got untied during the storm last night, and now she's in a strange place where she doesn't know any of the people, but they all seem to know her. Princess Adriana is very afraid."

Sam leaned into the sofa a little more, his shoulder rubbing Kelly's as he settled in to hear her story, which would, he was certain, amplify the same reassuring things she'd just told the kids. Family was wonderful, family mattered and family loved you no matter what. He also knew she'd add in a part about God being there for the princess as He was for the twins, to reinforce her message about God's love. Kelly never ended story time without assuring the twins that God loved them. Sam realized he didn't mind that one bit.

What a woman. What a perfect mother for the twins.

Sam wanted Kelly to stay. But was it only for the twins?

As his shoulder bumped hers and the soft, wispy fragrance of her coconut shampoo filled his senses, he let an image of the future play in his mind. A future with Kelly, here on the Triple D, sharing winter, summer, autumn and spring, watching the kids grow and each other age.

He'd never wanted a future with anyone but Naomi, and that was to be a future filled with travel. Yet in the quietness of this precious family time, the past faded. Sam didn't want to leave these dear girls. He didn't want Kelly to leave, either.

Maybe he could risk a future with Kelly. Not because he loved her. He would never allow himself to be that vulnerable again. But he did care for her a great deal.

Would plain old affection be enough for a generous, loving woman like Kelly?

Somehow Sam thought that mere *affection* would be cheating her. A woman like Kelly was meant to be loved for herself, because she loved everyone else.

And truthfully? Sam didn't know if he was capable of that kind of love again.

"So that's just a bit of what Australia and New Zealand have in store for you." Kelly smiled at the group gathered in Sheena's agency a month later. "I hope it's been helpful. It's a wonderful place to visit with so much to see that one trip won't be enough for you."

She blushed at the loud clapping and faked a bow.

"I'm sure Kelly would be happy to answer any questions," Sheena said as she stepped to the front. "Let's get some coffee and a snack, and you can ask her your questions. Then I want to tell you about the tour I intend to escort to Australia next year."

A unanimous "ooh" rippled through the room before everyone began chattering.

"Thanks, Kelly. You really whetted their appetites, and those picture books you've passed around are enhancing the attraction. I'll have to think of a way to thank the twins for letting me borrow them." Sheena would have said more, but a client interrupted and she turned away. Kelly spent the next ten minutes answering questions then headed for the coffee table.

"It was an interesting talk," her mother said from behind her. When Kelly turned she saw Arabella wearing a big smile. "I had no idea you'd been to New Zealand. As a child, I had a pen pal there."

"I didn't know that." Kelly poured a glass of juice, eager to soothe her tired throat.

"We still correspond even though we're both much older." Her mother dangled a tea bag in a cup of hot water. "We went through breast cancer together."

"What?" Kelly almost dropped her juice. "You had breast cancer? When?"

Shocked and appalled that she hadn't known, she drew her mother into a corner apart from the others and listened as her mother explained what she'd gone through.

"That's why I didn't want you to come home that time," she said. "I was going through chemo and I didn't want anyone to see me. I looked horrible. But I made it through that and radiation."

"Marina should have told me." Anger burned inside.

"She didn't know." Arabella shrugged when Kelly frowned at her. "I can't explain it. I just needed to get through it my own way. Your father was wonderful."

Kelly couldn't process the information, couldn't make the abandonment she'd felt then align with this new view. So she stood silent, listening as her mother shared insights she'd gained from her pen pal.

"I imagine you've wanted to visit her there," Kelly said, but her mom shook her head.

"We've talked on Skype, and I've often wished I could meet her in person. But I never really liked traveling very much," she admitted. "I like my home, having the security of my things around me." She looked directly at Kelly. "I guess that's why I never understood your wanderlust. I'm sorry I made it so difficult for you to do what you love."

Completely silenced by the apology, Kelly could only stare at her.

"You see, I always thought my daughters would live near me, that we'd stay in touch, together." A smile struggled to lift her lips. "When Marina married, I was scared I'd be alone. Then you left and confirmed my worst fear. It's taken a very long time and some talks with my new friend for me to accept the reality that I make enemies of the ones I love because I try to force them to be what I want. For that, I'm deeply sorry."

"Oh, Mom. I don't care about that. I love you." Kelly embraced her and held on, her heart singing at the abrupt about-face that had taken place. She didn't know why it had happened, but she praised God for it.

"You're probably what's changed me." Arabella chuckled when she drew away. "And Mayor Marsha happened. Marsha's become my dearest friend. We've shared a lot. She's the friend I've always wanted, and she's helped me see the mistakes I've made, how I must have hurt you all, trying to get my own way. She's been wonderful."

"Mom, I'm so glad." This answer to prayer was so unexpected that Kelly couldn't quite believe it. "I think moving to Buffalo Gap has started a new life for you."

"It has." Her mother's face suddenly fell. "I only wish Marina—"

"She knows, Mom, and she's rejoicing. As am I." She set down her empty glass, took Arabella's teacup, too, then folded her mother in her arms and held on, savoring the contact she'd craved for years. "I love you so much."

"I love you, too, Kelly. I never said that enough." Her mother clung to her, her lashes wet against Kelly's neck. When she finally drew away, remorse filled her face. "I wish you didn't have to leave, but I understand. That's your life and you love it."

Did she love it? Kelly wondered. As much as she once had?

"I just want us to have as much time together as possible before you go." Arabella smoothed her hair, touched her cheek, her smile radiant. She looked ten years younger. "Come see us and bring the kids. *All* of them," she emphasized. "Let's share the time we have. Your dad would love it and so would I."

"I'll come, Mom. I promise." Kelly hugged her again, unable to believe God had given her this wonderful gift of reconciliation.

"You'll be welcome, honey. You're our daughter, part of our family. We love you." Her mother wiped her eyes, completely smearing her eye shadow. Oddly, she didn't seem to care. "I have to get home. Your father wants to go for a walk this evening," she said with a tender smile. "He likes to check on the flowers in the park."

"Give him a kiss for me, Mom." Kelly clung to her hand for a moment before releasing it. Her mother turned away then turned back in a rush and enveloped her in a swift hug.

"Thank you for being so forgiving, Kelly," she whispered in her ear. "I love you. I can't tell you enough."

"Love you, too, Mom." Kelly watched her leave, her heart in her throat.

She glanced around. Sheena had prepared for this night for ages. Seeing her now, among her clients, her face alive, Kelly knew she wasn't needed anymore. So she slipped out the door and drove to the park.

There she sat in the car and watched her parents enjoy the spring evening as they wandered around the small area, stopping to talk to someone or touch a bloom. Her father held her mother's hand, and every so often she patted his cheek. Kelly had never seen them so happy together, as if the world around them didn't matter, as if they didn't need it because they had each other and that was enough.

Finally, tears streaming down her cheeks, Kelly started the engine and drove back to the ranch.

That was what she wanted. That was why she couldn't settle for a marriage that was for the twins. Because Kelly Krause wanted the complete package—a man who adored her, whom she adored. She loved Sam, yes. Loved him enough to refuse what he offered because she knew it would never satisfy her needy heart.

"Isn't there a way You can make Sam love me?" she prayed as she drove. But as always, she came back to the pivotal point in her faith. Trust. Not her will, but God's. "Help me be okay with that," she whispered.

Clinging to her faith, Kelly walked inside, ready to tell Sam about her mother. She stopped short at the sight of Abby seated at the kitchen table with Sam, a sheaf of papers spread in front of them, both faces grim.

"What's wrong?" She glanced from Abby's serious look to Sam's angry one, waited to hear the dreaded words.

"The Edwardses have filed their claim. You and Sam are

to appear before the judge at the end of next week, which is when he'll also talk to the children." Abby bit her lip.

"So soon? But that's not all of it, is it?" she whispered, reading the truth on Sam's haggard expression.

"No. The rest of it is that this judge is particularly inclined to favor married guardians who have the time, money and support to care for children," Sam growled. "We're going to lose. So where's God now, Kelly?"

Right here.

But she couldn't say it because fear had taken control of her world.

"It was every bit as bad as I said it would be, wasn't it?" Sam squeezed his fists by his side, silently imploring Kelly to tell him he was wrong.

"I don't think it went well," was all she could manage. She kept her eyes averted, staring blankly toward the end of the court building in Calgary.

Sam fought hard to keep his anger in check, only because he feared revealing the least bit of temper at the unfairness of this judge could seriously affect the kids' future. "Why doesn't God help?" he demanded.

"I don't know." She did face him then, her eyes filled with tears. "I'm scared, Sam. What if he decides the twins have to go? What do we do then?"

"What *can* we do?" There was a whole lot more he wanted to say, but Kelly's worried face, her trembling body and the fear anyone could see just by looking at her forced him into action. He drew her into his arms and held her close. "It has to be okay," he whispered into her hair. "Doesn't it?"

"I don't know," she said, voice muffled by his shirt. "I don't know."

They clung together, each trying to bolster the other

and both failing miserably. They drew apart only when the twins finally emerged with the court clerk and Abby.

"You should have the judge's decision soon. Certainly by July first," the clerk said, her eyes on Emma and Sadie as they wrapped their arms around Sam and Kelly. "Good day."

"It's not a good day," Sadie said to the clerk, her voice loud in the hallway. "And I don't like that grumpy man. My grandpas are lots nicer."

Sam wanted to clap at her temerity, but he didn't dare lest the clerk had some sway with the judge. He stood silent as she glared at him before she turned and walked back into the courtroom.

"I don't like *her*, neither," Sadie added, not quite under her breath.

Emma said nothing. But then she hadn't since the moment she'd been led inside the building. It had been clear from the judge's reaction when he'd cut short Abby's explanation of Emma's vocal issues that he thought Emma's behavior stemmed from something Kelly and Sam were doing wrong.

"I don't like it here." Sadie's hand tightened on Sam's, drawing his attention. "Can we go home?" she asked, gazing up at him with complete trust.

He didn't deserve that trust. He knew he was going to lose custody of the kids. Because he hadn't been able to trust God. Or because he wasn't a good enough father. Or something.

"Yes. Let's go home, Sam," Kelly whispered in his ear.

Home? As they walked toward the truck, Sam wondered, *Where is home if Kelly and the twins aren't there?* As if in a stupor, he stood mutely, clinging to the twins' hands, waiting while Kelly thanked Abby for all she'd done.

"Don't give up," Abby warned. "We've seen amazing things happen at Family Ties. If you think about it, God's already done a lot by bringing the twins to the Triple D and keeping them there. He has this in hand, too. He knows what He's doing. Trust Him."

Sam made sure the twins' seat belts were securely fastened, helped Kelly into her seat then drove toward the ranch.

Trust. He was so tired of hearing that word. He was sick of that sinking feeling in the pit of his stomach whenever he contemplated sitting back, waiting for God to do something.

What if He doesn't? a little voice inside him chirped. *God didn't do anything for Naomi. Why is this different?*

Like sediment building to create stone, that hardened part of him inside grew more resistant. God didn't need his trust. He'd do whatever He wanted, no matter how Sam pleaded for help.

Jaw tight, he drove, hearing the chattering voices around him as the twins, free of the gloomy atmosphere of the court and not really understanding what was at stake, begged Kelly to take them for a walk by the river so they could gather stones for the sandbox Sam had promised. Another thing Jake had wanted to make for them last year and hadn't had time.

"I need to do some chores," he told Kelly when the twins had raced inside to see their grandmother, who was watching Jacob Samuel. "Can you handle them alone for a while?"

"You have to ask?" She gave him a sad smile. "Of course."

"I won't be long," he promised. Her hand clamped on his arm before he could leave.

"Why is it so hard to believe that God could make something good out of this, Sam? Can't you put the tiniest bit of faith in your heavenly Father?" Kelly waited then sighed heavily when he didn't answer. "We'll be fine."

"See you soon." He turned to walk away, but once more her hand on his arm stopped him. Sam glanced at her hand then into her face. Her big brown eyes brimmed with tears.

"Please, Sam. Let go of the fear," she whispered.

He wanted to. He wanted so badly to be free of the heavy, clawing worry that dragged him down to despair.

"I can't," he said. "I have the same stone in my stomach that I had when Naomi died. We've lost the case, Kelly. We failed my brother and your sister. It's just a matter of time until you accept it."

"But God hasn't failed, Sam. God's still in charge, still working all things together for good. And while He's in charge, I'm not giving up anything."

Then she walked regally into the house. Heaving a sigh of frustration, Sam headed for his workroom in the shed and the change of clothes he kept there. Then he saddled his horse and headed for the hills after giving Oscar instructions.

He rode off knowing he couldn't afford the time away from work. He'd taken too many days off as it was because of the kids. Problem was, he couldn't afford not to ride as far as it took to find some solace, to keep from venting on someone. Oscar would care for the ranch. Kelly would care for the kids. Sam trusted her with them just as he'd trust her with his life.

He realized then that in all the horribleness since Jake's and Marina's deaths, Kelly was the one shining star, the one thing in his life he wouldn't change. Sam had only to be near her, to watch her with the twins or Jacob Samuel, and her contagious hope and optimism took over, for a while. One thing he *could* thank God for was Kelly.

He kept riding farther and farther into the hills, where people seldom came because the terrain was too rocky, the land too wild. Here his herd ranged for the best grass. Here the land remained untouched, the same as it had been a hundred years ago. Here he'd found solace before, but now Sam had questions. He needed answers.

"So what's my purpose?" he asked when he'd reached

the summit of an outcropping. "What am I here for?" Anger built at the hopelessness of his situation.

He glared at the sky, unable to remain silent.

"Every single dream I've ever had, You've taken. What do You want from me, God?"

Trust.

Kelly's words came back to him. *God's still in charge. And while He is, I'm not giving up.* Kelly trusted God.

"I can't. I feel like You're trying to trick me or ruin me. It's asking too much."

Trust.

"Everything would have been fine if Kelly had married me. We could have kept the twins then. Why didn't You work on her?"

Trust.

Sam kept throwing out questions, but that one word repeatedly hammered inside his brain.

Trust.

Exhausted, the sun dipping behind the hills, he rode home, his heart raw, his soul ragged.

Kelly said nothing as she set a warm plate of food before him. She served him fresh lemonade with ice and a piece of apple pie, smiled warmly at his thanks. But Sam thought she knew that every bite tasted like dust.

The only thing that warmed the ice around his heart was seeing her smile and kissing the twins and Jacob Samuel good-night. And soon two of those three would be gone.

Sam stood by Jacob Samuel's crib, smoothing a hand over his back as the baby slept. The thoughts that filled his brain seemed like those of a traitor, but he was as committed to doing his best for the baby as he had been for the twins, and the truth was unavoidable.

"Sam?" Kelly tugged on his arm, drawing him into the family room. "Come. Sit down and talk to me. Tell me what you're thinking about."

He sat down beside her, relishing the feeling of togetherness that being next to her always brought. But it wouldn't last, not when she heard him out. Sam couldn't say it. Not yet. When he didn't speak, she rose, walked behind the sofa and began kneading the taut muscles in his neck.

"Talk to me, Sam. You've always been able to talk to me."

Yes, he had. So now he told her of his thoughts.

"When you're gone and the twins are gone, I won't be able to manage alone. And I can't expect my parents or yours to babysit all the time."

"You don't know the twins will be going, Sam. But anyway, continue." She kept kneading, those kind, gentle hands of hers freeing the knots that had held his brain captive so that now his thoughts gained clarity.

"Even if I found a sitter who would come in, there'd have to be days off, times when I take the cattle to market," he said quietly. "There'd be days when I move the heard north, situations when day care just wouldn't cut it."

Kelly's fingers stilled. She walked around the sofa to stand in front of him, clenching her hands.

"What are you saying, Sam?" Her voice was barely audible.

"I think I might have to ask Abby to find a temporary family for Jacob Samuel," he said. The silence of the room was deafening. He looked up to find her staring at him in horror.

"You're willing to give away your own nephew? That's how little faith you have in God's love?" She shook her head, her eyes so sad it made his heart hurt. "I'm glad Jake and Marina aren't here to witness this. I don't think they'd ever forgive you. I don't know if I can."

Kelly turned and fled from the room as if she couldn't stand to be near him anymore.

Sam had never felt more alone.

Chapter Twelve

"**W**hat's wrong with Uncle Sam?" Sadie demanded two weeks later as she and Emma watched Kelly remove their bikes from the back of the truck. "Why isn't he coming to the Canada Day picnic?"

"He'll come later, honey." *Maybe*, Kelly thought. "He has to look after his sick horse."

Sadie and Emma looked at her with their bright blue eyes as if they knew she was making excuses for the uncle who seemed to have lost his laugh.

"It's almost time for the parade," Kelly told them as she set Jacob Samuel in his stroller. "I'm sure glad you two did such a nice job of decorating your bikes. They look wonderful. You remember what I told you?"

"Stay with the group and obey Auntie Abby's son, Ivor," Sadie chanted.

"And if you get tired?" Nervous at letting them go with the kids' bicycle group without her or Sam present in case something happened, Kelly told herself to trust God and stop worrying.

"We'll tell Ivor, an' he'll get someone to help." Sadie frowned. "I wish Uncle Sam was here."

So do I. Kelly struggled to suppress her longing as she pushed the stroller to where the other bike riders were assembling. She'd grown accustomed to having the big rancher by her side, imparting reassurance when she fussed about the kids, sharing the duties of caring for these precious children.

But Sam was still fighting an internal battle he couldn't win. In the process she felt he was withdrawing further and further from God—and her. Her heart ached to help him, but though she petitioned God constantly, they had not yet received news of the judge's decision.

"Okay, my darlings," she said now, hugging silent Emma then chatty Sadie. "Jacob Samuel and I are going to find a place to watch. We'll be waving at you." She checked that the maple leaf flags were still firmly attached to the bikes, ensured that Ivor would have water bottles if they became thirsty and that he'd bring the twins to her in the park when the parade was over, as he'd promised on the phone this morning. "Have a good time."

"Bye, Auntie Kelly." They waved for a moment but soon disappeared in the group of riders.

Goodbye. It was so hard to hear. Especially since yesterday Kelly had received an email from the cruise line reminding her she had a bit more than six weeks left of her furlough. Then she'd have to leave everything and everyone she loved.

Oh, Sam. Why couldn't you love me? her heart whispered. *I'm not Naomi, but I'm here and I'm alive and I love you.* She kept the smile pasted on her face as she passed new friends, who called a greeting. *This is home, Sam. If you're here.*

But as she found a spot in the shade to park Jacob Samuel, she tried to quash the yearning inside. God's will. That's what she had to focus on. What God wanted for her, not what she wanted. Her own desires had led her astray. Trusting God might cause some pain, but at least He wouldn't let her make another mistake.

Trust.

She gave Jacob Samuel a bottle and draped a blanket over the stroller to keep the light out, hoping he'd sleep for a while.

"Where have you been?"

"Sam! I thought you weren't coming." Her silly heart tap-danced with excitement as she gazed into his beloved face. She couldn't help looping her arm through his and pressing her cheek against his chest. "I'm so glad you did."

He wrapped his big hand around hers and squeezed. "I'm not missing anything else," he said cryptically.

Kelly didn't understand exactly what that meant, but she couldn't ask because the high school band came marching past, playing a tune that drowned out voices. So she stood beside him, reveling in the joy of being with him on this bright sunny day as they celebrated their country's birthday.

Sam must have noticed that she kept standing on tiptoe, trying to see if the twins were coming, because he leaned near her ear and said, "Relax, Mama. I checked on them before I found you. They're having the time of their lives."

She leaned her head against him. "So am I," she murmured.

Sam grinned and flopped an arm around her shoulder as the decorated red-and-white floats of local merchants rolled past. He roared with laughter when a clown grabbed Kelly's hand, drew her out of the crowd and made a big show of dancing with her before presenting her with a flower. A little embarrassed by the attention but enjoying the fun, Kelly accepted the flower, curtsied and let him lead her back to Sam.

"Didn't know you were such a good dancer," he said, his green eyes dark. "Are you going to save one for me tonight?"

"There's a dance?" she asked, her breath catching at the look he gave her.

"In the town square. We have one every year." He glanced away suddenly.

Kelly wondered if he was thinking of the times he'd danced with Naomi there. As quickly as the thought came, she tossed it away, determined to savor every moment of the next six weeks. It would have to last her a very long time.

"You can have every dance," she assured him, blushing under his regard. "If you want."

"Yeah," he said then grinned. "I do."

She could have married this wonderful man. Why hadn't she?

Because you're committed to living God's will, not your own.

"Here they come." Sam nudged her shoulder and pointed.

Kelly searched the group then smiled as the twins appeared on the bikes, pedaling at the same pace as the other kids while they searched the crowd.

Sam yelled, and that got their attention. Their faces glowed, and their grins stretched wider when they saw him. Sadie lifted one hand to wave and almost lost her balance. Kelly caught her breath and held it until the wheels had once more stabilized. Then she cheered, too.

When they disappeared from sight, Sam bent his head. "They did good," he said, his pride evident.

"Yes, they did. Because you had them practice." She smiled, reveling in just being with him. "I'm not sure they'd have had the courage otherwise. You're a good uncle, Sam."

"Just not a good enough father." For a moment his face lost its joy. But then he shook his head and once more became the doting uncle. "Their decorations stayed on, too. Not like some of the others."

Jacob Samuel's squeal for attention stopped Kelly's response but couldn't stop her bubble of pride. This man *was* the twins' dad, whether that grumpy old judge said so or not.

Sam fetched the twins, then they retrieved the picnic basket, found a cool spot under a big maple tree and enjoyed the picnic lunch Kelly had prepared. After that the afternoon was filled with kids' games, a bread demonstration from the clay oven at the nearby museum and a tour of the service group tents scattered around the park, which offered Sam's favorite.

"How many pieces of pie have you tasted?" Kelly teased Sam when he finally sprawled on the grass, replete.

"Only four," he said sadly. "I'll try more later. So far my favorite is the lemon from the Rotary booth."

"That was mine." Kelly chuckled at his frown. "Dad's a Rotarian, but Mom didn't have time to make her pies because they're trying to get the quilt finished, so I made four lemon pies. Only lemon pies were Dad's orders."

"And you didn't keep one?" Sam demanded, surging upward. He leaned forward with a fearsome look. "That's not nice, Kelly."

"I only had ingredients to make four," she said, leaning back from his hovering face, trying to understand why he was acting so oddly.

"Girls, you'd better tell Auntie Kelly what happens when I don't get my lemon pie." Sam glared at her, but a muscle at the corner of his lips flickered.

"He gets mad," Sadie shouted. She burst out laughing when Sam growled. "He has to have lemon pie."

Even Emma was grinning as Sam loomed over her, hands outstretched, fingers wiggling.

"You look like some kind of crazy bear," Kelly grumbled, growing more uncomfortable as he moved closer. "Everyone's staring."

"Pie," he growled. "Lemon pie. Must have pie. Argh."

Kelly laughed nervously. "Girls, what makes him stop this silliness?"

"Pie!" Sadie said. "Only pie. You have to get him some pie."

"I can't." Kelly glanced down at Jacob Samuel, who lay

asleep on her lap. A growl came very close to her ear. "Sam, stop it," she said, heart thumping so loudly she thought everyone must hear. Around her, people grinned.

He moved so fast she had no time to back away.

"I'll stop if you promise to make me pie," he whispered, eyes dancing. "Tomorrow."

"But I have to help Sheena at the travel agency—"

"Argh!" Sam's growl sounded louder than ever, and it attracted several more children.

"Fine. I'll make you a pie tomorrow. Now stop it," she insisted.

"Not one pie. Three pies. Apple, lemon and, uh, strawberry," he said.

"One pie. You'd better take it or leave it," Kelly advised him with a glare.

"Three," Sam demanded. His face moved to within an inch of hers. "Or I'll kiss you right here in front of everyone."

Did women still swoon? Kelly ordered her body not to show how much she wanted Sam to kiss her. "You wouldn't dare."

"I'd dare a lot, Kelly Krause." Then he leaned forward and planted a big smacker right on her lips.

Other women might not swoon, but Kelly did. Fortunately, she didn't think she gave herself away because her arms were around Jacob Samuel. She did lean forward into the kiss then, realizing what she was doing, ordered herself back.

When she opened her eyes, she found Sam's face mere millimeters away, eyes twinkling at her.

"Three pies," he repeated.

"Give him the pies, Auntie Kelly," Sadie yelled, laughing uproariously at his antics. "Give him the pies."

"Fine." Red-cheeked and utterly embarrassed to see the number of people gawking at them, Kelly only wanted this to end. But Sam deserved some comeuppance of his own. "You'll get three pies," she promised as she eased her hand free.

"Good." He sat back on his haunches, looking supremely satisfied with himself.

"And this," she added, so mad and eager for payback she acted without thinking, pulling him forward by his shirtfront and planting a loud smacking kiss on his startled mouth. "Now behave," she ordered in a voice only he could hear.

Her shame was multiplied when around them people began to clap.

"I'm going home," she said, her face burning.

"Nope. Canada Day is an all-day thing in Buffalo Gap. Nobody leaves early, especially not you." Sam bowed at the crowd then waved them away. He turned to her with a shame-faced look. "Sorry. I guess I got carried away."

"You think?" Kelly kept her head lowered so she couldn't see the sly looks from the town's busybodies.

"I just wanted to see the twins laughing again, carefree, happy. Like they used to be." Sam's quiet words chased away Kelly's irritation in a flash. "Let's escape all these looky-loos and go for a bike ride." He jumped to his feet and held out a hand to Kelly.

"I don't have a bike," she reminded. "But the girls have theirs."

"I brought Marina's and Jake's for us," he told her. "And I borrowed a baby seat for this guy." He lifted Jacob Samuel from her lap. "Come on, Kelly. Please? Let's make a memory."

With that comment and the twins chiding in the background, what could she do but agree? As they pedaled through town on their bikes, Sam leading then the twins, then Kelly, she thought the memory must have been God-sent just for her. The twins, giggling and laughing, Sam smiling as if he hadn't a care in the world—she wondered what had changed him from the taciturn man of the last few weeks.

They returned to the park for supper with their parents. Then a small band gathered and began to play. Here and there all over the park, people got up and danced right where they were. The twins did, too, swinging each other back and forth, squealing with delight when Sam twirled them round for a fast number. Even her parents danced, though her father stumbled for a moment or two until his brain caught the rhythm.

"You promised me a dance, Kelly. Mom and Dad will watch the kids." Sam held out his hand. Without a word, Kelly went into his arms, unprepared for the shock of sensation running through her when he pulled her close for a slow waltz.

"You're a good dancer," she said quietly, studying his face in the twilight. "Did Naomi like to dance?"

"No." He stared at her. "She preferred to listen to the music."

"Oh." Kelly couldn't think of one other thing to say, so she gave herself to the joy of the music, sharing it with Sam as they glided from one song into the next. A quick step seemed to go on forever as Sam caught her around the waist and swung her a little off the ground. Then she leaned and dipped, following his lead. By the end of it, she was breathless, but that didn't have as much to do with the dance as it did with her escort.

"You're a very good dancer," he said, "but then I guess you do that a lot on the ship."

Since he'd seldom asked her about her life aboard, Kelly studied him for a moment before answering.

"I dance some," she told him. "Mostly when the ballroom dance teachers have a student who needs a partner." Sam made a face and she laughed. "Yeah, like that."

"Wanna sit for a bit while we wait for it to get dark

enough for the fireworks?" he asked and she nodded, perfectly content to sit beside this wonderful man as long as he wished.

"Cold?" Sam touched her arm as if to check for himself then grimaced. "That was a dumb question. It was hot this afternoon but you never once took off your sweater. I'm starting to wonder if you're cold-blooded, Kelly."

With you around all the time? A woman would have to be cold-blooded not to feel some heat when Sam smiled at her like that, dimples peeking out.

"I should have brought another jacket," she murmured, trying to chase away those wayward thoughts about him.

"I have an extra quilt," her mother said, holding out one Kelly remembered from her childhood. "If you don't mind sharing."

"I don't mind." He looked at her, one eyebrow lifted in a question. Kelly nodded. Sam lifted the quilt and swept it over both of them. "There," he said and smiled at her.

That smile started a little fire inside and a few moments later, when the wind picked up and his arm went around her shoulders, Kelly began to wonder if this was a good idea.

Somewhere in the park, someone started a sing-along. The tunes were old then new, fast then slow. The twins sang along, their eyes drooping every so often. Jacob Samuel was snugly asleep in his stroller, and after a few minutes Sam persuaded the twins to join them under the quilt.

"I just want them near," he murmured to Kelly.

So did she. She wanted them to sit together like the other families in the park. She wanted that forever. But then the fireworks started, waking Jacob Samuel. Sam handed her the baby, and Kelly comforted him. Sam leaned in against Kelly as he made goofy faces to get the boy to laugh until finally he saw the flares of color and babbled and pointed.

"God's raining stars on us," Sadie said. "To show He loves us."

Kelly's eyes met Sam's, saw them widen, heard his breathy gasp. To her shocked surprise, tears glittered on the ends of his lashes.

"Sam? What's wrong?" Kelly touched her hand to his face, scared by the look of bare loss in the beloved green eyes. "Please tell me."

He turned his lips against her palm and pressed a kiss there, moving his hand over hers and holding it against him. Then he leaned in to whisper in her ear.

"The judge's decision came, Kelly. The twins are leaving a week from today. For good."

He dashed a hand across his eyes. Then with an apologetic smile, he rose and strode away into the darkness, a lonely figure with the weight of the world on his shoulders.

Oh, Lord. Oh, Lord, please.

Kelly sat alone in the darkness, three sweet, innocent children nestled against her as her heart wept for everything Sam had lost.

She wanted to pray. She desperately wanted to find the words to plead with God to ease Sam's shattered heart. But all she could pray was, *Why?*

He was a coward, Sam decided the following morning. A weak, sniveling coward to leave telling the twins up to Kelly. And yet some part of him insisted that she was the right one to do it. He knew he'd only mess it up, as he had everything else.

"You mean we're gonna *live* with them?" Sadie shook her head and folded her arms across her chest. "Not me."

Emma copied her actions, though she said nothing.

"But sweetheart, you'll have a wonderful time. Eunice and Tom have a lovely house, and you'll both have your own rooms. They have the sweetest dog named Hobo. You love dogs. And there's a pool you can swim in."

"A real swimming pool?" Sadie asked, eyes huge.

"Yes. With a diving board." Kelly had garnered the information from Abby and the report on the Edwardses, of which she'd received a copy. "They even have a bowling alley in the basement because Tom loves bowling."

"Is it fun?" Sadie looked dubious.

"Very fun," Kelly assured her.

Sam wanted to tell Kelly to stop when she went on ad nauseam about the wonderful home they were moving to. Not that he hadn't known what her approach would be. The two of them had stayed up all night talking, plotting strategy, trying to come up with the least painful way of telling the twins. Kelly had insisted they be completely honest but couch it in terms the kids could accept and with many assurances that both of them would keep in touch, something Sam fully intended to do.

The questions went on and on, but no matter how Kelly tried to wiggle around the truth, the twins were leaving, and they began to understand what that would mean. After an hour Sam called a halt.

"It's nice out," he said. "Let's go for a horse ride."

The twins jumped up and down, eager to resume the training Sam had started a month ago on a pair of little ponies he'd acquired just for them. He couldn't afford the time. He'd taken on too many fix-it projects, trying to build up his nest egg for the judge.

But now he couldn't afford not to. By next week, they'd be gone. Judging from that phone call he'd overheard last week, Kelly would follow soon after. And then it would be too late to do the things he wanted to.

"I'll stay here with Jacob Samuel," Kelly said, but Sam shook his head.

"He can ride with me in that sack thing you wear on

your shoulders. Marina used it," he assured her when she made a face. "He loves it. You'll see." She frowned and Sam softened his voice, appreciating her concern. "He's ten months old, Kelly. Soon he'll be walking."

She smiled, but it didn't reach her eyes. "Okay," she agreed finally. "Let's go."

Once they'd reached the meadow where he usually took the twins, Sam let himself relax and enjoy his little family. The twins were so precious, riding proudly in the small saddles he'd found online. What would he do with the ponies when the twins left?

"This was a good idea." Kelly checked on Jacob Samuel, who was grinning and waving his arms. "Everyone needed this. Thank you."

"I have a whole slew of things I want to do before they go," he told her quietly as the twins' horses followed the circular track through the long grass. "I want to make sure they don't forget."

"Sam." She touched his hand, her voice very gentle. "They won't forget you, no matter what happens. Once they've had time to adjust, you can go visit them. Abby said the Edwardses agreed to that. You'll still be Uncle Sam to them. Always."

"What will you remember, Kelly?" He watched her head turn as she gazed around her at the lush trees, the wildflowers growing in clumps all over, listened to the trickle of the now-dwindled stream. "When you're back in Timbuktu, sailing around on that fancy ship of yours, will you forget all about your six months on the Triple D?"

He waited on tenterhooks to hear her response, knowing it mattered a lot, yet unable to let her see that. Kelly's gaze returned to him, holding his with her liquid brown eyes. She didn't need words to express herself. Those eyes said everything if he could only understand it.

Her response to his kiss on Canada Day filled his head.

He didn't think she'd have kissed him back unless she felt something. But maybe that was sympathy.

"I've fallen in love with you, Sam."

He couldn't believe he'd heard right.

"Don't look so surprised. You're a perfectly lovable man. Sometimes." She chuckled, and it was like listening to wind chimes.

He was thrown off balance by her, confused and taken aback by her admission.

"I'm not asking anything of you, Sam. I know you don't love me. That's okay. It's not God's will. I've accepted that." Kelly shrugged. "Or I'll learn to. But I wanted to tell you. I wanted you to know that I care very much for you so that you'll understand that whenever I think of the time I spent on this ranch with you, I'll remember a man who held nothing back in his love for his family."

She leaned forward and tickled Jacob Samuel under the chin, laughing out loud when he crowed with delight.

"I'll remember seeing you at the airport and thinking I'd been reunited with a friend. I'll think of you at the funeral and remember how much you loved Marina and Jake, enough to give up your dream of travel to help them. I'll remember you with those two," she said softly with a nod to where the twins sat still as their ponies gorged on the fresh grass. "And with him. I'll remember you fixing anything that needed fixing to make life a little easier for all of us."

"Kelly—" His heart thundered in his ears at the tenderness of her words.

"I'll remember you on Mom's moving day, trying to get a fry before Dad ate it," she teased. He had to laugh but it died away as her face grew serious. "Mostly, I'll remember how you did everything you could for every single person who needed you, including me." She reached out to touch his cheek, a Kelly-type gesture he'd grown to adore. "I don't understand why God's allowing the twins to go, Sam."

"Me, neither," he croaked, surprised to find his voice didn't work.

"But I believe that somehow, some way, God will honor your love and generosity to your family. Because the twins and Jacob Samuel *are* your family, Sam. They always will be, no matter where they go."

He couldn't tear his eyes from hers. Finally, her hand left his face, touched his shoulder then dropped away.

"These upcoming days will be hard for you. I know that it's tearing you up inside to let go of the girls. But you haven't failed Jake or Marina or anyone else. They'd be so proud." She sniffed as a tear tumbled down her cheek. "When you get really down and you think you can't take any more, remember one thing, Sam Denver. You are loved. Not just by me but by God Himself."

Kelly leaned in and kissed him on the lips, asking for a response he could no more deny than fly to the moon. He couldn't quite believe that this wonderful woman cared about him, loved him. He didn't want her to go. He wanted her to stay with him, to figure out the future together. To raise Jacob Samuel, watch him grow to be the man his father wouldn't see. He wanted Kelly by his side when he visited the twins in their new home.

But Sam couldn't love her, couldn't allow himself to care for her. What if she got sick? What if God took her as He'd taken Naomi? Sam couldn't survive that.

So he drew back, breaking contact with the one woman who made him see possibilities, even when there weren't any.

"I'm sorry, Kelly," was the best he could manage, and Sam knew that was pathetic.

"I know." She turned, called the girls and together they rode back to the ranch.

All the while Sam's brain screamed, *Fool!*

Chapter Thirteen

Easing away from soft, pudgy arms that wouldn't let go, driving away while tears streamed down the twins' faces, their soft mewling cries ringing in her ears, nearly tore out Kelly's heart. But she kept her misery to herself as Sam drove them home, knowing that he was suffering just as deeply as she.

"They're only five," he said, his voice ragged, his fingers gripping the wheel. "And they've had three homes. It isn't fair."

"No, it isn't." What else could she say?

The rest of the ride was done in silence. When they pulled into the yard, Sam made sure Jacob Samuel and Arabella were all right before he disappeared. "To work," he told Kelly.

"The poor man." Her mother's gentle words were barely audible. "He loves them so much."

"We both do." Kelly had held it together as long as she could. Suddenly, she collapsed in a chair by the table, laid her head on her arms and wept her heart out.

"Oh, Kelly." Her mother patted her hair, trying to soothe her when nothing could.

"They were crying for us to take them with us," she sobbed. "Emma didn't say anything, but she didn't have to. You could see her fear in her eyes. And Sadie, oh, dear Sadie." She groaned at the memory she didn't want to have. "Sam thinks he'll have to find someone to care for Jacob Samuel when I go," she whispered. "Marina's baby that she wanted so much will be raised by someone else."

"Kelly." Her mother's pensive tone made her look up. "Why didn't you and Sam marry? I'm sure the judge would have let you keep the twins if you had."

"Abby told us there was no guarantee of that, particularly since the ranch doesn't have a lot of spare cash right now. Jake and Sam made a big payment to their dad when he retired, and then Sam used his money to cover Marina's treatments—" She stopped when her mother gasped.

"He what?" Arabella whispered.

"I shouldn't have said anything. Sam didn't want it known, but he paid for Marina to have two treatments that were supposed to help her have a baby. And she did. Jacob Samuel." She held out her hand so he could squeeze his fingers around hers and pull himself up from the floor.

"I had no idea." Her mother collapsed on a chair as if she'd had the wind knocked out of her.

"That's how generous he is. That's how much he loves his family," she said firmly.

"Yes, I see that now." Arabella fell into thought for a moment then lifted her head and studied her daughter. "I've known for some time that you've fallen in love with him," she said quietly.

"Yes," Kelly agreed. "But Sam doesn't love me."

Arabella frowned. "Are you sure? His actions seem to speak very clearly—"

"Sam's a nice man, Mother. He's nice to everyone. He gives and gives and gives. But he's been deeply hurt. His fiancée suffered with cancer and died. Sam blames God for letting that happen. He's never been able to get over her."

"I think he has," her mother said after a pause. "I think he loves you. He just doesn't know it or he's afraid of it."

"You're wrong, Mom." Kelly sighed and swung the baby into her arms. "I don't want to talk about it anymore. I'll be leaving in a couple of weeks. Is it okay if I bring this guy and come by a lot?"

"Darling, of course." Her mother hugged her and the baby. "We'd love that, your dad and I. This house will seem empty with the twins gone. Come and see us anytime."

"Where's Dad today?" she asked curiously.

"Marsha's husband has taken him fishing." Arabella tilted up her nose and leaned toward Kelly. "I know it's not nice, but I hope they don't catch anything. I don't want Neil cleaning fish in the house. He makes an awful mess."

Kelly burst out laughing and then the tears came and she couldn't stop crying. "Oh, Mom," she wept. "What am I going to do?"

"Pray," Arabella said staunchly. "And remember Who it is we serve." She smiled then quoted, "'Now glory be to God, Who by His mighty power at work within us is able to do far more than we would ever dare to ask or even dream of—infinitely beyond our highest prayers, desires, thoughts or hopes.'"

"That's quite a verse."

"Marsha taught it to me," her mother said proudly. "Think hard about those words, Kelly. Things may look hopeless to you, but God will use them, if you let Him."

"Thank you." Kelly hugged her again, so grateful that this woman was her mom. "I love you."

"The feeling is entirely mutual." Her mother giggled then grabbed her purse. "Are you working on a new picture?" she asked.

"I was making one of the kids for Sam but—well, I've put it away for now." She shrugged. "It would only bring him sadness."

"Bring it along when you come tomorrow. I'd like to

see it." Arabella hugged her once more, smoothed Jacob Samuel's hair then left.

Kelly watched her leave then with a sigh put Jacob Samuel in his walker and started supper. Then she called Sheena.

"I'm going to be in town tomorrow at Mom's. I could stop by your office and help you put together information on those brochures if you want," she offered, thinking how she'd never had to find work to fill her days, till now.

"I want," Sheena said. "Come when you can and bring the baby."

That was tomorrow planned, but what about the day after and the day after that? She stood at the window, hoping for a glance of Sam.

He'd said nothing after she'd told him she loved him. He'd thrown himself into doing things with the twins, but now that they were gone, would he notice her?

"I need to stop wishing for what I can't have, don't I, little one?" She swung Jacob Samuel into her arms and walked outside.

"By His mighty power at work within us is able to do far more than we would ever dare to ask or even dream of— infinitely beyond our highest thoughts or hopes." The thing was, Kelly was afraid to ask for what she most wanted, because she knew God's answer to her prayer for Sam's love was no.

She put the baby in his stroller and pushed it at a brisk pace down the road, needing to do something, anything, to get her mind off two small girls in an unfamiliar place, calling her name.

And of a man who didn't want her love.

Oh, Lord, her heart wept. *Help me help him.*

"Are you sure there's nothing I can do?" Sam demanded, knowing the answer. "But I've had several reports that the twins are not settling in at the Edwardses. They're not happy.

Surely the judge doesn't want to make children suffer by keeping them in a place where they're miserable."

The judge's assistant gave the same glib response she'd used the last two times Sam had called. "The judge is looking into it."

He cradled the phone with forcible restraint and caught Kelly watching him.

"They're not happy?" she whispered, her eyes dull.

"Abby visited two days ago. The twins have been there a week, and Emma's had a bad dream every night. Abby said the two of them drag around those airport dolls I gave them. Eunice can't seem to interest them in the tons of toys she has."

"The pool?" she asked then drooped when he shook his head.

"Abby said Sadie told her she and Emma pray every night that God will bring them home." Sam dragged a hand through his hair. "Why doesn't He help them? I'd prefer they went somewhere else, anywhere that would make them happy, even if it isn't here."

"I know." Kelly smiled sadly, sharing his pain.

"You haven't got much time left here," Sam pointed out when the silence stretched too long. "Just over a week?" He didn't need to ask. He knew exactly when she was leaving. And he was trying to hang on, to keep from begging her to stay. "Jacob Samuel will miss you."

Kelly made a noise he couldn't decipher. But he knew it was pain. He glanced around the room, thought how happy this house had been, how it was now a shell of sadness.

"I'm going to be working in the south paddock this afternoon," he told her. "The fences there have been neglected and need a lot of work. I won't be back till late."

"Okay. I might go for a ride with Jacob Samuel," she said quietly, her voice too soft, too aching. "I want to take a good look around that meadow where we were with the girls."

Before I go.

The words hung unspoken between them, as did her words of love. He'd never acknowledged them, Sam realized. And he couldn't now. Kelly might think he was asking her to stay. She might think he needed her help with Jacob Samuel, that he couldn't manage alone.

And all of that was true. But he wasn't going to keep her here, deny her the life she loved.

"Be careful," he said. "Take a cell phone."

"Will it work in that valley?" she asked.

"You might have to climb a hill in certain places," Sam admitted. He had to get out of there before he said or did something he would regret. "Kiss him good-night for me, will you?" he asked. It was getting harder and harder to watch Jake's son grow and change, knowing he couldn't keep him here, couldn't look after himself and run the ranch.

Why didn't— No! There was no point in going there.

"Bye."

Kelly said nothing, simply watched him go with those sad brown eyes. He could almost hear her say, "Trust God, Sam. He has a plan."

Yeah? Well, Sam didn't think much of a plan that let two young girls be miserable.

He clamped on his Stetson, forced away thoughts of the beautiful brunette in the kitchen and started loading his truck with fence supplies.

How would he stand the emptiness when Kelly, his friend, his confidante, the only woman who dared to call him out on his faith—how would he manage when she left his life, too?

How was it his whole world had fallen apart in six short months?

With the baby snuggled in his carrier in front of her, Kelly set off on the short ride to the meadow. All around her, the hills burst with green, alive, growing, changing. Full of promise. The exact opposite of how she felt on hearing news of the twins' sad state.

In the meadow she dismounted, lifted the baby down and set him on the quilt she'd brought along. She'd come here to try and make sense of her world, to sort things out, and yet nothing made sense.

Kelly loved Sam. She'd never been more sure of anything in her life. This love was like a glow inside her that wouldn't go away, even though she tried to pretend to herself that it wasn't there. She had only to look at him, and her dreams began. If only he loved her.

But it wasn't only Sam who had her confused. Since she'd been reunited with her mom and seen new signs of her father's decline, she'd been praying constantly for a way to reconcile her reluctance to return to the ship with her longing to stay and savor every moment she could wring before disease stole her father completely. Arabella would need her then, her support, her comfort, her help.

"And what of you, my darling boy?" she asked, watching Jacob Samuel crawl across the quilt. He'd be walking soon. How could she miss his first steps, his first words? How could she go back to her life, knowing this precious child would be raised somewhere other than his home?

And who would keep track of the twins, send them weekly updates about the princess on her ship? Would the Edwardses remind them of Marina and Jake, the parents who'd adored them? Would they cry because their aunt never visited? Would Emma ever speak again?

"Is it truly Your will for me to go back?" she prayed aloud, feeling close to God here in this beautiful land He'd created. "I want to stay more than anything, but how can I? I have no job, no way to support myself. Jacob Samuel won't need a caregiver forever. Then what? Please help me, God."

"Infinitely beyond our highest prayers, desire, thoughts or hopes," her mother had recited.

"You know my highest prayer is to do Your will, God," Kelly said. "But I also want to finally be a daughter to be counted on, a friend to those who've supported me, a help for Sheena, a parent for the twins, though that's impossible now." She squeezed her eyes closed for a moment then leaned back, the baby by her side, and gazed at the blue sky above. "I want to be the one to bring stability to Jacob Samuel's life, to be a substitute mom for him."

And then she spoke the rest of it.

"I want to be near Sam, even if he doesn't love me. I want him to see Your love in a new way. I want to watch it happen. Please?"

Heartfelt prayers spent, Kelly played with her sister's beloved son, holding his hands so he could toddle over the grassy field, laughing as he picked a flower and tried to eat it, showing him the many birds that darted here and there.

Able to do far more than we would ever dare to ask or even dream of.

Kelly stood up, her face heavenward, and said in a clear firm tone, "I'm daring to ask, God. I'm daring to ask You to lead me on a new road. I'm not going back to the ship. I'm staying where my heart is, where my family is. I'm daring to dream that You will give me the desires of my heart. I'm trusting that You will reach Sam and show him Your love."

The release of those words brought a solid peace to her heart. She'd learn, with God's help, how to live without Sam's love. But she wasn't going to stop loving him.

"Infinitely beyond our highest prayers," she recited as she folded and stored the quilt in a saddlebag. "Infinitely beyond my desires or thoughts, Jacob Samuel." She kissed his silky cheek then fixed him in the carrier on her chest. "Infinitely beyond my hopes," she said as she swung herself up on her horse.

To show her faith, she began singing the doxology. But the mare took only a few steps before she stopped and refused to move. Kelly dismounted, tugged on the reins and saw the horse was lame.

With a sigh of disgust she pulled out her phone, only to realize she'd forgotten to charge it. The phone was dead.

"Not very bright of me, was it, little one." She took down the quilt and spread it once more on the grass. "I don't want to hurt the horse. We'll have to wait here for Uncle Sam."

She had no doubt he'd come for them. Sam cared for those he loved and though he might not love her, he dearly loved this sweet child in her arms. He would move heaven and earth to get to them, no matter how late it was.

And it was growing late. The sun had dropped beneath the mountaintops. The evening was cooler. Kelly had already put Jacob Samuel's jacket on and tied his little hood. She'd fed him his snack earlier. Now she had only one bottle left. She checked her watch and knew he'd soon be screaming for food. Once it was gone…

She did everything she could think of to placate the baby, and when he began demanding his food, she fed him only half the bottle. Though he wanted more, she tucked away the rest. Who knew how long they'd be here before Sam came?

Dear Sam. Kelly pulled the quilt around her and let herself pretend it was Sam's arms that held them, Sam who protected them.

"Please God, help Sam see Your love in a new way," she whispered. "He needs Your peace so badly."

With Jacob Samuel nestled against her, she watched the stars emerge one by one, amazed by their brilliance and beauty.

Hurry, Sam. We need you. I love you.

Chapter Fourteen

Sam frowned when he drove into the yard and saw Kelly's mother sitting in her car.

"Arabella," he said when she jumped out and hurried toward him. "What's wrong?"

"I don't know, but I can't reach Kelly," she said, her face as white as her shirt. "I've been phoning her since six. It's ten now. Where is she? Where's Jacob Samuel?"

I might go for a ride with Jacob Samuel. I want to take a good look around that meadow where we were with the girls.

"Where's my daughter, Sam?"

"She was going for a horseback ride." He swept past her, hurried inside the house. Everything looked as it had earlier. "She took a cell phone," he said, noticing its absence.

"I've been calling it. There's no answer. Something is wrong, Sam."

He stared at the worried mother, waiting for her diatribe to begin and knowing he deserved it. He should have gone with Kelly. He eased past her and out the door to ask Oscar to saddle two horses.

"Kelly and the baby are missing," he explained. Oscar, face grave, hurried to saddle up.

"You know where she is?" Arabella asked.

"If she's still there. She was going to the meadow where

we took the twins." Sam assembled a bag while he spoke, trying to cover every eventuality. Food for the baby, a bottle of formula and some water. A couple of treat bags left over from the twins' birthday in case Kelly was hungry. A first-aid kit.

"You think she's hurt? Or the baby is?" Arabella asked, fear in her voice. "Oh, Lord."

"Yes, pray for them, Arabella. Pray hard." There was no choice but prayer now. Sam grabbed several flashlights. "Where's Neil?"

"Marsha's with him. She'll stay as long as she needs to. Sam?" Arabella grasped his arm, tears streaming down her cheeks. "You have to find them. I can't lose Kelly or Jacob Samuel. It's bad enough that the twins are gone. We can't lose them, too."

She wept harder, though he tried to comfort her.

"I need Kelly. I've missed her for so long. I want her to stay, to be with her dad and make up for what she's missed. I need her to be with me when—when things get worse." She brushed away her tears and peered at him. "You love her, Sam. I know you do. Please bring her back here where she belongs."

"I don't love—"

"Yes, you do. I've seen it in the way you are with her. You're fooling yourself if you pretend you don't love her. And she loves you." Arabella managed a smile. "My daughter is no idiot. She fell for the most handsome man in town, but also the most wonderful. I'll never be able to thank you for helping Marina. But Marina's gone now." She hiccupped a sob. "I don't want to bury another daughter, Sam. Please find Kelly and bring her home. She belongs here, with you. You and that blessed baby."

He pulled her into his arms and held on tight. Trust Arabella to get to the heart of the matter, he thought as he marveled at what he'd been blind to for so long.

"I do love her," he whispered, feeling the glory of it fill his heart and soul. "I never thought I could, but she's the reason I keep going, keep trying, even though the twins aren't here anymore. It's for Kelly," he said in wonder.

"Of course it is." Arabella drew away and smiled. "Kelly fills our days with sunshine and hope. She's our gift from God. Love is always a gift from God." She patted his back. "I'm going to make some soup for when you bring her back."

His brain fogged by the idea that God had given him love for Kelly, stunning Sam. He'd been looking at God as if He owed it to Sam to do what Sam wanted. But God was his Maker, the Maker of the universe. As a parent, He knew what His children needed. Who was Sam, a mere man given the opportunity to live in the kingdom, to set himself as God's judge? How foolish he'd been.

"Forgive me?" he asked silently, swimming in a wash of shame. "I didn't realize how stupid I was. You are God, the Lord of all. You don't need me to say what's right and what's wrong." Humbled, he bowed his head. "I accept Your decisions because I know You are love."

As relief fille dhim, he felt as if he could breathe again. How he wished Kelly was here so he could tell her.

God has a plan, Sam. He wants to give us our heart's desires.

His heart wanted Kelly. He needed her to make sense of his world. Without Kelly— Fear gripped him in a wave so strong he swayed.

What would happen if God took Kelly?

For a moment sheer terror held Sam immobile. Then he weighed the grief of losing her with the dreadful emptiness of never telling her how much he loved her, and the decision was made.

Sam was going to cherish every precious moment he could spend with Kelly, no matter how long it lasted. And he'd thank God for the opportunity to love her for as long as he was alive. Because when he came right down to it, without trust in God, his life was utterly bare.

"Pray, Arabella," he said and yanked open the door. "Pray hard."

"Always, Sam," she promised with a smile. "God bless you."

"And you." He hugged her tightly, kissed her brow then left.

By the light of the full moon, Kelly saw the last few ounces drain out of Jacob Samuel's bottle. The little boy tugged hard then wailed when no more was forthcoming.

"I'm sorry, baby," she whispered, smoothing her fingers against his brow to check if he was warm enough now that a chilly wind had picked up. "That's all there is. You're such a sweet boy. Uncle Sam is coming. God's showing him the way. Don't give up."

Waiting here like this, it was like waiting to learn God's will. You needed patience and perspective. You needed faith.

Sam's coming. She told herself the same thing a thousand times, over and over, sometimes silently, sometimes aloud. She said it so often she almost missed the gentle plod of horse hooves on the stony path.

"I'm over here, Sam," she called as her soul lifted in praise. "We're over here."

A moment later she felt herself folded into the embrace of the man she adored.

"Oh," she gasped. And then she couldn't say anything as Sam kissed her, thoroughly, completely, adoringly, only stopping when Jacob Samuel protested very vocally. "He's hungry, Sam. I didn't bring enough food."

She blinked when Sam handed the baby and a full bottle to Oscar and asked him to feed the boy. Oscar smiled and happily set to work, humming a little tune as he did.

"Thank you for coming, Sam. I—" He kissed her again. And again. "Um—"

He pressed his fingers against her lips. "I love you, Kelly."

She blinked. Maybe she was dreaming.

"I love you so much." He kissed her eyelids, her nose and her lips once more and then grinned.

"Um, Oscar—"

"Knows exactly how I feel. He's listened to me for the past half hour." Sam chuckled. "I love you. Aren't you going to say anything?"

"It's such a lovely dream," she sighed, leaning against him and closing her eyes. "Don't wake me up. I want to see how it ends."

"With you marrying me and living here on the Triple D. With us watching Jacob Samuel grow and change and love God."

"Wait a minute. You love God?" She blinked and opened her eyes, touched his face. "You love God, Sam?"

"More than I ever knew. And I finally realize He loves me, too, though why He does, I can't fathom. I've been an idiot." He grinned and hugged her. "I'll tell you the whole story in a minute, but first there's someone who wants to talk to you." He dialed his phone and held it out.

"Hello? Mom? Oh, I'm so sorry I worried you. I'm fine. So's he. The horse went lame, that's all. I thought it might do some damage if I rode him, so I waited for Sam." She smiled at the stream of questions her mother kept asking. "I'll tell you all of it later, okay? Thank you, Mom. See you soon." Kelly hung up and handed back the phone. "Tell me," she said.

She listened, her heart singing praise as Sam told her of all he'd learned, of the grace he'd received and of his momentous decision to trust God with the future.

"I'm glad," she whispered, kissing his cheek and snuggling her face against his big, solid warmth. "I'm so glad, Sam."

"Yeah, me, too." Sam paused a moment, obviously waiting for something from her. Kelly raised an eyebrow. "Well," he grumbled, "how do you feel about me?"

"I told you, Sam," she whispered with a quick glance at Oscar, who appeared to be snoring as loud as Jacob Samuel, except she knew he was faking when she saw his eyelids lift for a quick glance around.

"Could you tell me again?" he begged. "Please?"

"I love you, Sam Denver. I love the way you care for those you love. I love your compassion and generosity. I love the way you keep giving, no matter what. I love you for caring for my sister and my parents and me. I love you." She peeked through her lashes. "Satisfied?"

"Not nearly. Maybe in sixty years." He kissed her tenderly, sweetly, his love clearly evident. "Kelly, what do you think about getting married?" He touched her cheek, grazed his hand down her jawline. "Not to make a home for the twins. I think that's finished. Not even to make a home for Jacob Samuel, though I hope we will."

"Then why?" she asked. But she knew. Her heart surged with joy as Sam explained.

"Because I can't imagine my world without you. You and I belong together, Kelly. Don't you think?"

"Yes, as a matter of fact, I do. That's why I decided tonight that I wasn't leaving Buffalo Gap. I'm going to strengthen my bond with my mother, share fun times with my dad, watch Jacob Samuel take his first steps and say his first words and all the other firsts. And I'm going to love you until you wish I'd sailed away on that boat."

"Not a chance," he promised.

"I always thought God didn't want me to have a family, to belong anywhere. Now I realize He had you in mind all along. All He asked me to do was wait for Him to work things out so His will could be done."

She touched his face, her fingers sensitized to every beloved dip and rise.

"You gave me a home and my family, Sam. You fill my days with joy. Nothing I ever found in any exotic place in this world can compare to the happiness I find with you on the Triple D. Yes, I'll marry you."

Sam gave a whoop of joy that startled both Oscar and the baby. Then he swung Kelly in his arms until she was dizzy. But when he kissed her, well, then she was in full possession of all her faculties and she kissed him right back.

"God's going to do something wonderful for us, Sam," Kelly told him as they rode home hand in hand, Oscar leading the way, lame horse following. Jacob Samuel slept in front of Kelly.

"I just wish the twins—" Sam gulped and smiled at her. "No, I'm leaving them in God's hands. He's the only one qualified to parent them."

Then they talked about a possible wedding date. Sam's only stipulation was soon.

When they reached the ranch, Kelly asked, "Sam? What do you think about me becoming a partner with Sheena in the travel agency?"

"Do you think you have enough experience?" he asked, tongue in cheek. Kelly's giggle echoed across the valley.

Sam stopped their horses then lifted her off hers and handed hovering Arabella the baby. Kelly would have followed her mom and Oscar, but Sam stopped her.

Kelly silently waited.

"I'm beginning to see," Sam murmured as his arm slid around her waist and he turned her to watch the first thin rays of a new day.

"See what?" she asked, squinting to get a better look.

"How God works all things together. It's perfect." He leaned his head against hers and sighed.

"I agree."

"When we get married, will you make me apple pie every day?"

"Sam!"

Chapter Fifteen

"I'm glad you didn't wait," Arabella said one week later. "You and Sam have been through so much. As long as you're certain he's the one God's chosen for you, there's no reason not to get married."

"No one could be more certain than me." They hugged, then Kelly turned to get another look at herself. "It's a gorgeous outfit, Mom. I can't believe you made this in one week. It's exactly what I wanted for my wedding dress."

Kelly gazed at the perfectly fitted jacket of white silk that hugged her figure to the waist and ended in a flared peplum. The long tulip skirt grazed the tops of her white satin pumps. Tiny embellishments of seed pearls dotted the outfit, matching the pearl-studded netting on the hat that covered her head and the veil cascading halfway down her back.

"I feel beautiful," she whispered.

"You are beautiful, Kelly." Her dad handed her the armful of red roses. "Sam sent these. He said red is your favorite color."

"And you are my favorite dad." She hugged him, checked her image once more then smiled at her mom. "I'm ready."

"You're only a few minutes late." Arabella touched her cheek, soaking in the sight of her daughter as if she couldn't get enough. "I love you, Kelly. I'm so glad you're finally home."

"Me, too." She hugged her mom then urged her parents out of the dressing room. "Let's get down that aisle before Sam changes his mind."

"As if," Sheena snorted as she led the way out of the dressing room to the aisle that led to Sam. She preened when Kelly complimented her on the autumn-toned maid of honor dress she'd chosen. "Jacob Samuel's wearing a tux," she whispered.

Kelly glanced up to see and got caught up in Sam's loving gaze. *Thank You, God.*

After one glance at her face, Sheena straightened, prepared to start down the aisle. Kelly slid one hand through her father's arm and the other in her mother's then took one step forward. She faltered when the church door opened and a familiar voice yelled, "Wait, Auntie Kelly!"

Sadie and Emma raced up to her then froze. "Wow," Sadie whispered. "You look like a princess."

"A princess," Emma whispered.

Kelly knelt and hugged them both, her heart overflowing with love.

"That's the first time Emma's spoken since you brought her to our house," Eunice Edwards said tearfully. She turned to her husband. "I knew this was the right decision."

"What decision?" The groom strode down the aisle. "What's going on?" Sam grinned as the twins embraced his legs and then oohed over Jacob Samuel. He straightened when Pastor Don cleared his voice. "Sorry, Pastor, but we have to get this straightened out," he apologized to the minister, who still waited at the front. "What decision?" he asked Eunice.

"We're moving back," Sadie crowed. Emma nodded and grinned.

"Tom and I are canceling our petition to adopt. We realize now that the twins belong with you, on the ranch. You and Kelly are their family. Not us." Eunice gulped and started to move away.

"That's not true." Kelly was so proud as Sam moved forward to stop them. "You are family. You and Tom have done exactly what family does for each other. You put the twins' needs ahead of your own wants." He took Kelly's hand in his and squeezed. "We can't thank you enough for that."

"We had to." Tom smiled at the twins. "We can't stand to see them so sad. We'll get out of your way now." He took his wife's arm, but Kelly protested.

"You can't go now," she said. "Sam and I are getting married, and we want all our family present."

"Please do join us," Arabella added, her smile beaming.

The Edwardses finally agreed. As the usher guided them into the sanctuary, Eunice said, "You see, Tom, I was right. I knew those two were in love. It was just a matter of time."

"Can we get married, too?" Sadie asked. "We're fam'ly."

"You certainly are." Kelly beckoned to Sheena. "The girls will walk down the aisle first, then you, then me. Okay?"

"Absolutely perfect," Sheena said.

It seemed everyone agreed. As soon as Sam took his place in front with the baby, the girls skipped down the aisle, beaming at everyone. Sheena went next.

Kelly lifted her head and met Sam's gaze. She could feel the love emanating from him. With her parents by her side, she took her first step, her soul rejoicing as her mother recited in a clear firm voice,

"Now glory be to God Who by His mighty power at work within us is able to do far more than we would ever dare to ask or even dream of."

Pastor Don led them in their vows, reminded the community of their duty to help the couple and finally told Sam he could kiss his bride. Kelly stared into her husband's eyes, her heart brimming with joy. When he didn't immediately kiss her, she frowned.

"Kel—" he squeezed her fingers, his voice low enough that only she could hear "—I'm sorry, but I think we'll have to cancel our honeymoon trip to Banff."

"Oh, no, Sam," she said, grasping his lapels and pulling his head closer. "We're not canceling, we're postponing, until we can make it a family holiday."

"You know I've kind of lost my yen for travel," he said, smoothing his knuckles against her cheek. "God's put all the world I need to see right here in this church."

"Me, too." She smiled, deliriously happy. "But I think our family should see at least some of their world. Don't you?"

"Isn't Uncle Sam gonna kiss her?" Emma demanded in the clearest, loudest voice Kelly had ever heard.

Kelly blinked away a tear of joy and smiled at Sam. "You heard the child."

"Yes, ma'am. I surely did hear her. Clear as a bell." He kissed Kelly in a promise meant to seal the rest of their future, the one God had worked out for them.

* * * * *

Keep reading for an exclusive excerpt of
THE RAIN SPARROW by
New York Times *bestselling author Linda Goodnight.*

Available now from HQN Books!

Dear Reader,

I'm so glad you came back to Buffalo Gap, where friends are always welcome and babies and quilting are the norm. I hope you enjoyed Kelly and Sam's story. It's sometimes hard to trust in God's presence and His will. Kelly thought she'd never belong, and after trying to get her own way, found more than she ever imagined on the Triple D, including a reunion with the mother who ordered her not to come home.

Sam is one of those men who don't stop giving; the Fix-erator. But even he couldn't fix it so that the twins he adored could stay on his ranch. Only when Sam stopped trying to run the world and handed it back to God did he get the solution he craved and the woman he loved. Love is an awesome power in the world. We need more of it.

I'd love to hear from you. Write to Box 639, Nipawin, SK, Canada, S0E 1E0; email loisricher@yahoo.com or visit my webpage at www.loisricher.com.

Till we meet again, I wish you the strength to welcome obstacles as opportunities, the courage to stand steady during uncertainty and most especially the security of God's sustaining love through every trial and every joy.

Blessings,

*Lois
Richer*

A mystery writer and a shy librarian find love on a dark, stormy night in Honey Ridge, Tennessee...

BARE FEET SOUNDLESS on the cool tile flooring, Carrie moved to a pantry and removed one of Julia's sterling silver French press urns. "We'll have to grind the beans. Julia's a bit of a coffee snob."

"Won't the noise disturb the others?"

Thunder rattled the house. Carrie tilted her head toward the dark, rain-drenched window. "Will it matter?"

"Point taken. You're a lifesaver. What's your name?"

"Carrie Riley." She kept her hands busy and her eyes on the work. The fact that she was ever-so-slightly aware of the stranger with the poet's face in a womanly kind of way gave her a funny tingle. She seldom tingled, and she didn't flirt. She was no good at that kind of thing. Just ask her sisters. "Yours?"

"Hayden Winters."

"Nice to meet you, Hayden." She held up a canister of coffee beans. "Bold?"

"I can be."

She laughed, shocked to think this handsome man might actually be flirting a little. Even if she wasn't. "Bold, it is."

As she'd predicted, the storm noise covered the grinding sound and in fewer than ten minutes, the silver pot's lever was pressed and the coffee was poured. The dark, bold aroma filled the kitchen, a pleasing warmth against the rain-induced chill.

Hayden Winters offered her the first cup, a courteous gesture that made her like him, and then sipped his. "You know your way around a bold roast."

"Former Starbucks barista who loves coffee."

"A kindred spirit. I live on the stuff, especially when I'm working, which I should be doing."

She didn't want him to leave. Not because he was hot—which he was—but because she didn't want to be alone in the storm, and no one else was up. "You work at night?"

"Stormy nights are my favorite."

Which, in her book, meant he was a little off-center. "What do you do?"

He studied her for a moment and, with his expression a peculiar mix of amusement and malevolence, said quietly, matter-of-factly, "I kill people."